Gunsmoke Mountain

When wealthy Wyoming rancher Amos Corbett's beautiful daughter is abducted, Dan Featherskill is offered the job of finding her. Although he is a skilled mountain man and known adventurer, Dan turns down the job. Something does not ring true, and besides, Corbett wants him to swear to kill Celia's abductor. Dan may be a lot of things, but not a bounty killer.

Three hardcases are set upon the trail and when they threaten the high country ranch of Deucie Campbell, the mountain girl who once gave her heart to Dan, he has no choice but to take a hand.

And then a winter storm grips Shadow Peak and all hell breaks loose across the timberland.

Gunsmoke Mountain

Owen G. Irons

A Black Horse Western

ROBERT HALE · LONDON

© Owen G. Irons 2006
First published in Great Britain 2006

ISBN-10: 0-7090-8093-X
ISBN-13: 978-0-7090-8093-0

Robert Hale Limited
Clerkenwell House
Clerkenwell Green
London EC1R 0HT

Typeset by
Derek Doyle & Associates, Shaw Heath
Printed and bound in Great Britain by
Antony Rowe Limited, Wiltshire

ONE

The quiet dusk had faded to the blue of night. The Wyoming sky was moonless, the earth was damp and dark. The fitful breeze was filled with the sharp scent of mountain sage and the rich smell of mown alfalfa. The shadows of the oak trees surrounding the farmhouse were as black as coal. The man with the drawn Colt revolver waited, crouched and motionless. Starlight cast crooked shadows before him as he moved to the open window of the house. The gunman parted the curtains with the muzzle of his pistol, threw his leg over the sill and slipped into the room.

Celia Corbett came instantly alert at the small sounds the gunman made as he crossed the wooden floor to her bed and placed his hand over her mouth.

'Be silent and everything will be all right,' the man told her. She nodded her head slightly. Her startled eyes could not make out the intruder's face, but she knew who he was. She knew there was no point in arguing with him.

Celia swung her bare feet to the floor. She had fallen asleep before undressing for bed and she was fully clothed in range dress except for her boots. She tugged these on as the gunman watched the bedroom door, the thin ribbon of light bleeding into the room at its base, listening for any sound. The girl rose from her bed in silent surrender.

'There's two horses outside,' the shadowy man told Celia. 'You go first. I'll be right on your heels. Don't make a sound.' He gestured toward the window with the Colt.

Celia hesitated. 'Why are you doing this?' she asked, but the man was impatient.

'This is no time for questions.' He glanced again toward the door, believing he had heard a small noise beyond it. He said in raspy command, 'Now! Let's get going. Do you understand me?'

Celia could only nod, snatch up her hat from her nightstand, slip outside under his watchful eye and walk through the shadows toward the waiting horses. She knew better than to speak now, knew better than to do anything but obey as the man swung into the saddle of the other horse and motioned to her.

She heeled her horse and the animal started to walk away from the house, its hoofs silent against the damp, heavy grass, taking her away from the only home she had ever known as the grim rider beside her followed in silent escort.

The man issued his demand with cold bluntness. 'You find the kid that stole off with my daughter. If she's alive, you kill him and bring my Celia back. If she's dead, you kill him and leave him where he lies.'

'You're talking to the wrong man,' Dan Featherskill said softly.

The big man seated across the round saloon table scowled even more deeply. He was wild-eyed with anger and Dan's words did nothing to soothe him.

There was an untouched mug of beer near Featherskill's elbow. Now he picked it up, studied the man over the rim of the mug and took a sip. 'I'm not a bounty hunter, Mr Corbett.'

'It's not bounty huntin'!' the big man said roughly. 'It's retribution.'

'That's not my specialty either,' Featherskill shrugged. 'Sorry, Corbett, but this is not my line of work.'

'You don't understand!' the big flat-faced man said so loudly that men lined up along the bar turned their heads. Amos Corbett leaned forward, thumped a thick finger on the scarred surface of the barroom table and said in a lowered tone, 'Celia is all I have. She has to be found!'

Dan Featherskill studied the bulky man's eyes carefully. It was difficult to tell if Corbett was more liable to erupt in anger or burst out in tormented tears. His leathery face, sun-lined and sagging with the weight of the years and with sorrow remained set with insistence. 'You have to find her, Featherskill. You don't understand . . . look,' he said fumbling in his jacket pocket, 'I have a picture of Celia with me. I brought it so you'd know her when you found her. Look at her face! That sweet, sweet face.'

Featherskill looked at the daguerreotype Corbett placed in front of him without interest. He saw the image of a slender, fair-haired girl, not pretty but nice-looking in an amiable way, seated in a high-backed, ornate chair. She was wearing a fancy white dress with ruffs at the cuffs

8

and neckline. In one hand she held a rolled document – some sort of school diploma, Featherskill guessed.

'How could you not feel for me?' Corbett asked, his hound-dog eyes studying Dan's. 'To lose my daughter!' He slid the picture back across the table and slipped it into his jacket pocket.

'I do feel for you,' Featherskill replied, taking another sip of his beer, 'but I'm not the man for the job.'

'You're the only one,' Corbett said, clenching his meaty fists tightly. 'Look, Featherskill, you know the law won't help. The town marshal won't go beyond the city limits, the sheriff won't step over the county line without a wanted poster in his pocket.'

'You're a big rancher,' Featherskill pointed out.

'And it's round-up time! You know what that entails, Featherskill. I've got three men left on the home ranch.' He ran stubby fingers through his thick dark hair. 'One of them's thirteen years old, one's got a wooden leg! I can't raise a posse on my own. If I could, there's none of them know those mountains. You do!'

Featherskill was silent. Corbett was not listening to his replies. Dan felt for the man, understood his concern for his abducted daughter, but Corbett's anger led him to insist on one stipulation Dan could not agree to – he would not track down a man for the purposes of killing him. Whoever the man was he deserved a fair hearing.

'It's Shadow Mountain he's headed for,' Corbett said. 'They tell me you know that area like no other man besides the Cheyenne Indians.' Featherskill only nodded noncommittally, and an infuriated Amos Corbett continued. After taking a deep breath to calm himself, he added, 'There's no white man I've heard of who knows that area well at all.'

'You're right, I do happen to know the area,' Featherskill admitted. He tried to explain once again. 'I'm willing to try to find your daughter, Corbett, try to bring her home to you—'

'Then we're in agreement!' Corbett said, leaning back in his wooden chair with relief.

'Please let me finish! I will not shoot down a man out of hand.'

'Then hog-tie him and bring him back to me so that I can do it.'

'No.' Featherskill shook his head definitely. 'I will not. If he forces it, I'll kill him if I have to, but I won't do murder for you,' he said. Corbett's dark face grew darker with suffused blood. Featherskill had to put one more point forward. 'Do we know that Kyle Handy kidnapped your daughter? In the night without her making a sound? From her own bedroom?'

Corbett's eyes grew intent with anger. 'What are you saying, Featherskill?'

Dan's shoulder lifted in the merest of shrugs. 'Youngsters have been known to run off together before this.'

'That would never happen! Could not. You do not know Celia!'

'No,' Featherskill said to the offended rancher, 'I don't, and that's just it, Corbett. I'd have to know her. I'd need to talk to her. If I were to find out that she wanted to be with Handy—'

'She's only a child! It could never happen the way you suggest,' Corbett said, in a challenging tone.

Dan Featherskill met the man's hostile gaze evenly; he lifted his beer and finished it. Pushing the mug aside, he rose.

'You have to understand, Corbett. However certain you may be, I am not. With no disrespect to you or your daughter, I just can't know what happened with certainty.' Dan picked up his hat

11

from a nearby chair and planted it on his head. 'I can't be hired to do murder, Mr Corbett.' Not even for $800, which was what Corbett had offered him.

Corbett opened his mouth but said nothing. He knew he had failed, and his heavy lips moved only in silent curses as he watched the lanky man with the low-riding Colt pistol on his hip stride from the room, pushing through the saloon's batwing doors to emerge into the bright, cold sunlight of the Wyoming morning.

Dan stood before the saloon for a minute, twisting the points of his small mustache tighter. The lines around his eyes deepened as he smiled to himself. Well, that was that. One more job he might have had, lost. He had better find a way to make some money soon. He wasn't going to spend a Wyoming winter on the range, and his hotel bill had reached the margin of his resources. Highslip had offered him a job as deputy marshal, but the idea of breaking up fights, tossing drunks out of saloons or serving eviction papers on impoverished squatters as a way of life rubbed against Featherskill's lifelong tendencies.

He had determined early on in life that he would live free. He worked when he pleased and chose jobs that seemed either important or pleasant to him. Corbett's vicious little offer did not suit at all. Nor did Marshal Highslip's. Wearing a badge was much like wearing an anchor. Dan Featherskill had worn one for a time. Dan respected the law, but he could not accept the rigidity of it. He was inclined to make his own determinations where guilt and innocence were involved, and the law viewed such laxness with deep disapproval.

The wind was cold and gusting. The muddy, rutted street was dotted with iron-gray pools of water. Featherskill crossed the road, lifting his eyes to where the thrusting peaks of the Antelope Hill Range stood, shrugged off by the Rockies. He could not see Shadow Mountain itself, but in his mind the image of its craggy reaches was clear.

He entered the stable where his black horse stood looking at him curiously over a stall's partition. It pawed the ground underfoot impatiently. It seemed the animal had rested enough and needed some freedom of its own.

'Taking your horse out today?' Charlie Wheatley asked. Featherskill turned to see the scrawny stable hand, leaning on a pitchfork, standing in the shadows of the barn.

'He needs to stretch his legs.'

'Be more than a stretch, wouldn't it?' Wheatley asked, his small eyes narrow with cunning.

'Doubt it. I don't feel like riding for long. It's downright chilly out,' Featherskill said. He picked up a wisp of hay and hand-fed the black, rubbing its strong glossy neck. Wheatley was an idiot, he reflected, but he kept his horses well.

'You mean you're not going toward the mountains?' Wheatley asked. He removed his hat to scratch his thin patch of red hair. At Featherskill's frown, Wheatley shrugged and said, 'I sure would – for eight hundred dollars. That is, if anyone was to ask.' He smiled crookedly. 'Which they won't.'

'Everybody knows everything around here, it seems,' Featherskill said, turning back to face Wheatley.

'Just about. I mean everybody knows Corbett is looking for a tracker. He's been bellowing around town for two days now.'

'Everyone even knows that he's offering eight hundred dollars for the job?'

'I heard it,' Wheatley said, without amplifying his remark. Featherskill busied himself saddling the black, smoothing the striped Indian blanket

14

over its glossy back. Sunlight fell in bars through the chinks in the slat siding. The stable smell was full but not overpowering. Across the stable a palomino lifted its head and looked intently toward the double front doors. Dan glanced that way as well.

Two men wearing range clothes, carrying Winchester rifles, strode deliberately into the stable leading two weary-looking horses. Wheatley, wiping his hands on a rag, went to greet them.

'Good morning, gentlemen,' Wheatley said. The taller, narrower of the men, a blond rider, declined to answer. The shorter, swarthy man with him muttered a greeting. 'What can I do for you?' Wheatley asked, and there was a tension, as of nervousness, in his high-pitched voice now.

'Rub 'em down and grain 'em,' the dark man said. He removed his gray hat, wiped back his sparse dark hair and let his eyes shift to study the stable's interior. Seeing Featherskill he touched his companion's sleeve and nodded.

Alone, the dark man strode to where Featherskill had slipped the bit into the black's mouth and was now tightening the twin cinches of his Texas-rigged saddle.

'Is your name Featherskill?' the dark-eyed

man asked. His shirt was open at the collar, showing a mass of dark curly hair, and his hand rested on the butt of his revolver nestled in its silver-pinned holster. Dan halted what he was doing and let his eyes lock with the stranger's.

'That's right,' Dan said without inflection. The stranger's eyes narrowed and he studied Dan from head to foot.

'You're out of this, understand? You won't need your horse.'

'I don't believe I know what you're talking about,' Dan told him, kneeing the black to force the air from it as he tightened a cinch strap. 'I need my horse when I want it.'

'You won't be riding into the mountains,' the stranger said, taking half a step forward. Beyond him, in the sunlight falling through the double doors, Dan could see the second rider shifting his Winchester as Wheatley eased away uncertainly.

'My pony needs some exercise,' Dan said, 'that's all I'm doing. Now, if you'll get out of the way?'

Stubbornly the dark-eyed man held his ground until Dan began leading the black out of the stall. Its frisky spirits caused its legs to lift vigorously and the rider had no choice but to back away.

Dan walked to the doorway, his hat tugged low, leading the black. The blond man watched him, glancing once toward the other stranger as if for a signal. Yet he made no move and Featherskill emerged into the cold light of day and swung aboard the black without incident. He walked it toward the edge of town, the black taking a notion to prance sideways. Looking back, Dan saw the two strangers standing in the doorway, watching him.

No matter. He didn't know who they were, or want to know. You crossed the paths of men like that every day in rough country. They could be drunk, mistaken, showing off or just plain stupid.

Oddly, Dan didn't believe those two were any of those.

The black was in fine fettle on this brisk morning, and it trotted forward eagerly, straining at the reins. Dan let it run then, streaking across the long gramma grass-covered flats. Here and there violet lupins grew in clusters and fading patches of black-eyed Susan. It was late in the year and they would soon be no more, but they still prospered on this morning. Dan slowed the black and allowed it to splash over a narrow rill. The stream, a wandering vein of Willow Creek, was too small to be named, too shallow to be a hazard, too erratic to be utilized. No Name Creek was just an afterthought of some mountain storm.

They had now ridden a mile from town and Dan held the heavily breathing horse to a walk as they wound through a grove of live oak trees, passing through to the irritation of a rising flock of raucous crows. Pausing in the cool, heavy shade Dan looked westward. Now he could see Shadow Mountain, its peak wreathed in drifting clouds, fragile, sheer and twisted. He studied the timbered slopes and rugged crags for a long minute, remembering. Then, a little roughly, he turned the big black horse's head homeward.

Dan had returned to the stable after an hour and was rubbing the black horse down. The animal nibbled at the hay in its bin, muscles still quivering beneath its obsidian hide. Wheatley had wandered over to the stall. He watched Dan silently as he curried the black.

'Who were those two men?' Dan asked, without turning to face the stableman.

'The ones you were talking to?'

'That's right.' Dan paused, and turned his eyes toward Wheatley, noticing the apparent strain on the man's face. The stable man glanced toward the double doors before he answered.

'The dark one, the one doing the talking, was Brad Feeley. The other's Dallas French, the Trinidad gunman. I suppose you've heard of them?' Wheatley enquired hesitantly.

'I've heard them mentioned,' Featherskill said, replacing the currycomb on its hook. 'What makes my business any of theirs?'

'Amos Corbett,' Wheatley said.

'Oh, I see. The reward.'

'That's right, Dan. I heard them talking after you left. They were here to talk to Corbett. They know about the eight-hundred dollar reward. They heard that you were after it too.'

'I see.' Dan shrugged and put his hat on. 'Well, they've talked to Corbett by now. They know that it isn't true. I've no interest in the job.'

Relaxing, Wheatley said, 'I'm glad to hear it, Dan.'

'Why? What difference could it make to you, Charlie?'

'Dan – they said they would kill you if you got in their way. They mean to have that money if it takes murder to get it.'

On the way back to the hotel, Dan thought about Wheatley's words. 'If it took murder' – well, that was what it would take apparently, the way Corbett had laid out the job. Not Featherskill's murder, but that of Kyle Handy. Dan wished he knew something more about the boy. It might be that he was just a young man foolish in love. If every man guilty of that was killed the population of this planet would be dramatically reduced.

He wondered if he should talk to the marshal, but John Highslip was undoubtedly aware of what was going on around him. Everyone else seemed to know. Dan shrugged the notion off mentally. There was going to be trouble before this was finished, but he was not going to be involved in it if he could help it.

Or so he thought.

But trouble was already waiting for him in his room.

TWO

The man waiting for Featherskill when he opened his hotel-room door had a Henry repeating rifle across his lap. He was round-faced, round-bodied and slope-shouldered. His hat was tugged low as he leaned back in the wooden chair in front of the window where sunlight through the sheer blue curtains painted an irregular trapezoid on the plank flooring.

Featherskill paused, one hand still on the doorknob, the other holding the brass room key. The round man wasn't asleep, Dan knew that. He tossed the key onto the bureau and put his hat on the foot of the bed before speaking.

'Nice of you to come visiting, John.'

The man in the chair shifted and now light falling through the window glinted off the silver star that Town Marshal John Highslip wore pinned to his red shirt. The lawman tipped back his hat and tilted his chair forward.

'Hello, Dan. I hope you don't mind that I just let myself in.'

'I don't mind,' Dan said, seating himself on the sagging bed. 'It just makes me wonder why I'm so honored.'

'I didn't want to talk to you any place we could be overheard,' the stout marshal said intently. 'Everything that's said becomes common knowledge in this town. Word spreads like fluff from a cottonwood tree at seeding time.'

'I've noticed,' Dan said. 'There's not a person in town who doesn't know that I talked to Amos Corbett about his troubles this morning. And turned him down.'

'That is what we have to discuss,' Highslip said. Dan frowned as Highslip braced himself and rose from the chair, leaning his rifle against the ill-papered wall beside him. 'You are going to have to get involved in this matter, Dan.'

'I am not!'

'You are,' Highslip said gravely. 'I can't believe you would leave that girl in danger like she will be.'

'Miss Celia has help on the way,' Featherskill

said, yawning. Highslip put a friendly but firm hand on the tracker's shoulder.

'I'm not talking about the Corbett girl, Dan. Don't you see? It's Deucie I'm talking about!'

'Deucie?' Dan blinked up at the marshal. The big man loomed over him, dark and bulky before the sunny window. 'What does Deucie Campbell have to do with this?' Featherskill asked with a laugh. 'Never mind!' He held up a hand. 'I don't think I care to hear anything about her.'

'The hell you don't! You're going to, Dan. Like it or not.' Highslip's hand fell away from Dan's shoulder and he turned to walk to the window to stare out at the cool, bright day, toward the distant mountains which surrounded the long valley.

'You don't understand about me and Deucie,' Dan said to the marshal's vast, flabby back.

'The hell I don't!' Highslip said, without turning around. 'I was there that day, remember? The day she told you to get out of her sight and never show your face again. I recall you said something clever back to her like *never* would be too soon for you.'

'I was short on originality that day,' Dan said, trying to keep his tone light.

'To my mind you were short on brains that day, Dan,' Highslip replied. He walked back toward the chair, thought about sitting, but didn't. 'No matter what happened out there then, you can't let her fall into harm's way. She's in danger, Dan,' he said severely.

'What do you mean?' Dan spread his hands. He kept his features blank, or so he thought, but his heart was racing. Deucie in danger! 'How?' he asked the lawman.

'The word I get is that those two runaways – Kyle Handy and Celia – are heading toward Shadow Mountain. What is out there, Dan? Nothing. Not a trading post, not a mine camp. Nothing but the Campbell ranch. That's where they'll have to go. For shelter, supplies, directions . . . right to Deucie's place.'

'That could be, but—'

'It makes more sense when you realize . . . Dan, are you telling me you didn't know that Deucie is Celia Corbett's cousin?' The marshal was frowning down at Dan Featherskill. Dan was a little shaken. Surprised at the least.

'No, John, I didn't know that. Wait – how could she be? I knew Deucie's mother and father both. Beth Campbell, she died when Deucie was no more than ten, but I recall her. Thurston! He and I used to go elk hunting each fall. Deucie didn't have a cousin that I ever knew of.'

'You know that Thurston married again after Beth passed on. A year or so back.'

'Yes.'

'Roxanne is her name.'

'I didn't know that. I haven't been out that way since Thurston died . . . and me and Deucie had that trouble.'

'I know that, Dan. That's why I'm trying to tell you how things are. Roxanne and her brother, Amos, drifted into this country a couple of years back. Roxanne worked in town for a while and then hitched up with Thurston Campbell. Most folks didn't care much for Roxie, but Thurston was pining for a wife, and no one ever heard of her doing him wrong. She and Deucie seemed to get along all right.

'So she married herself a widower. Funny,' Highslip said, 'so did her brother. Amos Corbett married the widow Traylor, that is.'

Featherskill frowned deeply. 'Wait a minute, Susan Traylor was—'

'Celia's mother. Amos Corbett is her stepfather. Celia took her stepfather's name.'

'I didn't know that.'

'Of course not, you and Buckley were off trading lead in that Sweetwater River range dispute for most of a year. Anyway,' Highslip said with a deep sigh, 'that's how things are. Celia and Deucie aren't blood cousins, no more than Corbett is Celia's blood father, but they are sort of related by marriage. Them two used to ride together, go to church socials and dances and such. Deucie always introduced Celia as "my cousin, Celia".'

'I see,' Dan said thoughtfully.

'Do you? Now you tell *me* where Kyle Handy and Celia are riding? Especially if they have it in their minds that they're eloping.'

'That's not what Corbett thinks.'

'That's not what Corbett *wants* to think. He'd rather hire a pair of gunmen to track them down and bring Celia back kicking and screaming, preferably with Handy left in a shallow grave so it can't happen again.'

Featherskill put his hands behind his head and lay back on the bed. Looking at the ceiling, he said, 'This puts a different slant on things all right. If you know all this, John, why aren't you riding out to cut them off?'

'Three reasons, Dan – horses don't like me anymore' – he patted his ample bulk – 'and I don't like riding them; and I've got no authority outside of the town limits and you know it; third, I have a responsibility to my town. I won't have it turn into another Faverville.'

Featherskill knew what he was referring to. The Faverville town marshal had passed away and rather than elect a new one, the citizens of that town had decided they preferred things as they were. *En masse* they had gotten drunk, lawless and crazy enough to burn down their own town completely in the absence of authority.

'That leaves you, Dan,' the marshal said in a low voice. He picked up his rifle and cradled it under his arm. 'If you care anything about Deucie, you'd better start your pony toward Shadow Mountain. Because those two kids are surely riding that way, and they've got two very tough badmen on their trail.'

Dan watched the marshal cross the room heavily and go out, closing the door behind him.

If I care anything about Deucie? Deucie had been the most important thing in his life. She had meant everything to him . . . was that years ago or just moments? Deucie. That slender blonde laughing mountain girl. His Deucie.

Old Thurston Campbell had planned his whole life thoroughly. He would build a ranch in those rugged mountains, live happily there with his wife, Beth, and raise three boys to follow in his footsteps. Being something of a card player, Thurston had decided he would name his sons Ace, Deuce and Trey. He only planned on three sons, so there was no consideration given to what sort of an odd name the fourth boy might end up with.

But plans are one thing and life another. Campbell's ranch in that rocky, winter-tormented country had never prospered. It was all they could do to provide for themselves up on Shadow. Then Campbell's firstborn, a boy, had died in infancy. After another year of surviving the blizzards and the wild things, and one more birthing, Beth had surrendered to the wilderness and passed away, leaving behind Thurston and the one little baby: a girl. Deucie.

It hadn't needed any real consideration; Featherskill had been packing his saddle-bags even as he was mentally reviewing the past. He shoved a face towel, a razor and hairbrush into one of the leather bags. Unbuckling the other side he jammed in two boxes of .44-.40 cartridges, his spare revolver wrapped in protective oilskin, and a heavy sweater. He took his buffalo coat from the hook on the wall and shrugged into it. He glanced around the room. There was nothing else of his in it. The saddlebags now held just about everything Dan Featherskill owned in the world. And the face towel belonged to the hotel.

At least he wouldn't have to worry now about how he was going to pay next week's bill.

There was enough silver money in Dan's pockets to purchase a few items: sugar, salt, baking powder, cornmeal, coffee, some tinned fruit and potted meat. These he carried slung over his shoulder in a canvas sack to Wheatley's stable.

Wheatley, who had been standing near the ladder to the hay loft with a pitchfork in hand as if trying to summon the energy to clamber up, looked at Featherskill with surprise and said, 'I thought you weren't going to do any long riding, Dan.'

'Things have changed,' Dan answered bluntly. He saddled his horse again, getting a curious glance from the black. A little exercise was fine, but this looked to the horse like serious business.

Dan cinched down and tied his bedroll and supply sack behind the saddle, using piggin strings carried for that purpose. His canteen was full, but the water was old and he dumped it out, intending to refill it at No Name Creek. Then, taking the reins to the black he led it toward the double doors, looking toward the cold skies and the thrusting peaks of the far mountains. Unnoticed by him, three men had entered the stable while he was saddling. Now they stood in a row, staring at him as he approached the doors. Wheatley stood there motionless, rigid with worry.

'Friends of yours, Charlie?' Dan asked, as one of the men stood over to partially block Featherskill's way.

'Never seen 'em before,' Wheatley answered, his voice dry.

Neither had Featherskill. They were fresh from a long ride, that was obvious from their beards and trail-dusty clothes, but they were not men he might have met down on the Sweetwater during the range war or anywhere else on his past trail. A second man moved into the path of Featherskill and his horse.

'Your name Featherskill?' one of them, a narrow, red-bearded man asked, in a deep voice.

'Could you please step aside?' Dan answered. His eyes took in the three of them. No, he did not know them and didn't want to, but they seemed too curious about him.

'I asked you a question,' asked the red-bearded

one, the belligerent rider, stepping forward. Dan saw the man's hand drop toward his holster and he moved first.

Wheatley was still standing stock-still on Dan's right and Featherskill's hand snapped out and tore the pitchfork from the stablehand's grip. He took one lunging step forward and drove the butt end of the handle upward hard into the stranger's belly, catching him just below the joining of the ribs. The blunt force drove the wind out of the man and stunned his heart. He stepped away, doubled over and then fell to his face.

Another stranger, a balding ape of a man, started to draw his gun, but Dan's Colt was already up and leveled, the curved hammer drawn back, ready to fall with deadly result.

'You men don't need those guns. Drop them.' Dan's voice was soft, but the Colt's command was loud and clear. The two unbuckled their gunbelts and let them fall to the earth. They stepped away at Dan's gesture. Their friend still writhed on the stable floor, his breath coming in short whistles.

Featherskill mounted and kneed the black horse and it walked out smartly into the sunlight. Behind him one of the men lunged for his pistol, but the other said, 'Not now. We'll meet him later – out where there is no law.'

The breeze was mild but there was a chilling edge to it as Featherskill guided the black through the foothills at the base of Shadow Mountain. There were deep pines here and in the darkness of their shadows little could be seen. Now and then he spooked a deer and once startled a badger, but there were no human beings to be seen, nothing of their habitations or improvements.

Not that someone hadn't been here ahead of him. He followed the tracks of two horsemen for a part of the way. He assumed these were those of Dallas French and Brad Feeley. He knew they were men, for one of them had the habit of spitting his tobacco at small targets, a twig, an anthill, a rock at intervals.

Featherskill veered a little southward, not wanting to ride up on the gunmen. Although he would be forced to detour through a rocky, treacherous gorge known as the South Pass, the black was nimble, and he would be able to make better time than the outlaws would. If possible he wanted to get ahead of the two gunmen before they could reach the Campbell ranch.

Featherskill was assuming that Corbett, too,

had guessed the destination of his stepdaughter and her abductor. Or boyfriend. That was yet to be determined.

Reaching the foot of the South Pass which was a long, treacherous switchback leading through a field of granite sloughed off the peak's shoulder, Featherskill stopped, tipped back his hat and gave the black a little breather, looking down into the declivity of the gorge from which the broken trail rose to the heights. There, severe flash floods raged when the early rains came. Dead trees lay stacked like jackstraws in the depths of the canyon. Then glancing upward he took a determined breath and started on.

He had ridden only twenty yards or so before he saw the marker.

Frowning, Dan reined in and swung down from the horse's back. The wind was gusting strongly up the gorge, pressing at his back. The strip of red cloth tied to the branch of mountain sage fluttered and twisted in the wind. Dan snapped the twig and studied the cloth. What was it doing there?

The rag effectively marked the head of the trail. For someone unfamiliar with Shadow Mountain, the entrance to South Pass was invisible to the searching eye. Someone had tied this strip of cloth, torn from a garment, here as a guide. And it had to be a woman who had done it, Featherskill guessed. The cloth was silk and he had never seen a man in rough country wearing a scrap of silk.

The woman, of course, had to be Celia Corbett.

Dallas French and Brad Feeley, strangers to this country, were riding the far slope up and around the peak of Shadow Mountain. The only way that appeared open to travel. But Celia would know of the south trail. She and Deucie had ridden together, Marshal Highslip had told him. If she had ridden to the Campbell Ranch, Deucie would have used this trail which saved miles. So Celia knew of the trail and had marked it.

Dan frowned, looking down the long wooded eastern slopes toward the empty flats below. For whom had the marker been left? Possibly for her father, he thought, if Celia had indeed been abducted and was trying to mark a trail for her rescuers.

Dan swung aboard the black and started ahead, moving slowly through the field of loose shale and broken granite where nothing but an occasional, stunted cypress grew. He considered the matter further. What about those three rowdies he had met in the stable? Who were they? He doubted that Corbett had hired two crews to find Celia. Nor would Dallas French and Feeley have taken on more men. Theirs was a two-man job and they would have no wish to split the reward money into smaller shares.

And so. . . ? Dan was at a loss to explain matters. The only other person who might have tied the marker onto the twig was Kyle Handy. If that were so, why would he want to be followed? Dan put his conjectures aside. His thoughts were muddled, as dense as the gray clouds which were now lowering in the darkening skies, scratching their bellies on the ragged peaks. Errant wisps of cloud broke free and twisted and turned above him as well as below where they briefly masked sections of the long canyon. With a little imagination the tattered clouds became sorcerers' robes or haunting gargoyles. More than anything else, Dan thought, as he guided the black upward through the dismal damp of the day, they resembled one thing. *Gunsmoke.* Drifting past him with raw menace.

Dan looked again at the strip of red cloth he still held and stuffed it into his pocket. Then he rode higher through the cold settling mist that wreathed the mountain top.

The trail underfoot was roughly strewn with broken rock, but the black moved nimbly through it. The low clouds had dampened its pitch-black coat and dew dropped from the brim of Dan's hat. There were sounds in this wilderness – the occasional slap of a gust of wind against unyielding stone, the whining shiver of the twisted cypress trees as the wind tortured them again, the steady clop of the horse's hoofs and a distant moan as of a yawning god, indicating approaching thunder.

But there were no man-sounds, and for that Dan was grateful. Perhaps there was to be no trouble at all. Perhaps Highslip had been wrong in his conjecture. Perhaps the cloth was only a coincidence and Celia and Handy had made their run toward Denver or Cheyenne. Perhaps he would find nothing at the Campbell ranch but the ageing Roxie still sitting in her rocker before the fire and Deucie. Deucie alive and beautiful, cocking her head in quizzical anticipation, smiling as he rode the black up to the log house.

Then sound returned, racketing down the rocky slopes, and it was not the roaring of restless, waking storm gods, but the unmistakable man-thunder of gunfire.

THREE

The timber at the head of the trail was deep, dark and sheltering. Dan rode through the pine forest carefully, his hand resting on his holstered gun's butt. A woodpecker worked in the upper reaches of a lone cedar tree and a pine cone fell, just missing him. The black horse's head came up suddenly and Dan felt its muscles tense as it tried to stretch out to a quicker gait.

'Take it easy,' Dan muttered. He knew what had stirred the horse.

All animals have a memory and it recalled the little grassy meadow onto which they now emerged from the trees. There was still a sprinkling of blue gentian across the mostly dry grass and the thin rill still snaked its way tentatively across the meadow.

The horse recalled this grassy place as did Dan Featherskill. But he had last seen it in summer's warm sunlight when the grass had been long and lush. The horses – his and Deucie's – had grazed peacefully, their saddles stripped while he and the blonde-haired girl had eaten from a picnic basket and laughed together, stretched out on a blanket while an eagle circled effortlessly in the high crystal-blue sky above the mountain. . . .

Long ago.

Dan had allowed the horse to halt and it nibbled without evident enjoyment at the flattened brown grass of autumn. Dan patted the black's strong neck and said, 'I'll find you some good graze up ahead. This is mostly gone . . . mostly gone.' The ridge ahead of Dan was more lightly wooded, and more old cedar grew tall and thick among the pines. The ridge was formed in the shape of a crescent, and it sheltered the Campbell cabin from the north winds. Dan rode up toward the crest, keeping his eye on the land below him. He could now see the Campbell farm and a corner of the house.

The house was of log and stone. In the shape of an 'L', the front, smaller portion contained a living-room and the great native stone fireplace built to accommodate four-foot logs. The longer portion contained a kitchen and dining-room which one came to first going down the hall, then two facing bedrooms in the rear. Dan noticed no smoke rising from the high-shouldered chimney. He saw no extra horses in the yard, though they could be sheltered in the small, slab-wood barn or hidden in the trees.

No one was near the house nor in the fields where corn and alfalfa, neither looking in better shape than the other, had been planted, abandoned now for the season, apparently. Nearer the house was a vegetable garden, well tended, the rows neat and green with plants Dan could not identify at that distance. Drawing his Winchester from the saddle scabbard, Dan started the black down through the trees toward the log house.

He walked the horse across the dusty yard, past the well where a wooden bucket sat. He was in plain view from the house, he knew, and so he rode with caution, his grip tight on the Winchester. He heard no birds singing, saw no sign of farm animals. There was one white chicken watching him from the wooden porch of the cabin; now it turned and strutted off, head bobbing on its scrawny neck.

The door to the cabin was flung open and

there stood Deucie.

She stepped out onto the front porch, closing the plank door behind her. Her blonde hair was worn in a single heavy braid, the front chopped off in a pale fringe falling nearly into her corn-flower-blue eyes. For a moment Featherskill felt physically stunned, his throat constricted, unable to move for the sight of her loveliness, but he forced himself to concentrate, walking the black nearer to the porch.

'You can just ride out of here, Dan, you're not wanted around this farm.'

'I was just wandering around out this way, Deucie,' Dan answered. 'Wondered how you were.'

'You haven't wondered before, Dan,' Deucie said flatly, 'and you've been back for a long while.'

Featherskill was leaning forward, his rifle loosely held in one hand. He seemed to have all of his attention on the young woman, but his eyes were also taking in the windows of the cabin and he now saw a flicker of movement as some-one lifted one corner of a curtain to peer out.

'You heard me, Dan!' Deucie said. 'I asked you to clear out.'

Dan didn't reply at once. He was watching

Deucie's eyes steadily; he knew her too well for this transparent scheme to work. Her eyes did not show anger, but fear. Their depths sheltered an unspoken concern that she could not voice.

'All right, Deucie,' Dan answered. He thrust the rifle into its scabbard, lifted one leg over the black's neck, kicked free of the other stirrup and slid to the ground to face her. 'Just let me take your hand once and I'll be gone. For old times' sake. That's really what I came for, you know.'

'Dan. . . .' Deucie could only utter that single stammered word. Then Featherskill had stepped up onto the porch and with one arm he swept Deucie out of the way before he kicked in the door and rolled through into the interior, his Colt drawn.

Dan came to his feet directly into the face of a young man holding a rifle. He supposed this was Kyle Handy, but he didn't ask. Dan's right hand, still holding the Colt, slammed down into the young man's skull just above the ear and the stranger collapsed to the wooden floor with a thud. A woman's voice was screaming.

'You'll kill him! Don't hurt him, you savage!'

Celia Corbett – he knew her from her picture – looked as if she were going to hurl herself at

41

Dan tooth and nail, but instead the girl, clad in black jeans and a red silk blouse, slumped to her knees beside the fallen man, placed his head gently on her lap and bowed her face to his while she stroked him, cooing gentle words.

Deucie had come in. She stood against the bright rectangle of the open doorway.

'Shut that door and drop the bar,' Dan said, and Deucie complied without question. Now Dan noticed movement across the room and his eyes flickered that way, but it was only the old woman, Roxanne Campbell, her thin gray hair draped loosely across her shoulders, rocking furiously in her chair, her birdlike eyes fixed on Dan, her toothless mouth hanging open. She jabbed a bony finger at Dan and her mouth moved, but no words issued.

'She's had a stroke,' Deucie said quietly. 'She can't speak any more. She's telling you to leave Celia alone.'

'I have no intention of hurting her,' Dan said, looking at the old woman in the black dress and white knitted shawl. Then, to Deucie, 'I didn't want to hurt the young man here – Kyle Handy, is it? – either, but he had the drop on me with that Henry repeater. I had no way of knowing what his intentions were.'

'I know,' Deucie said in that soft, composed voice of hers. She glanced at Handy who now had awakened with a groan, watching them with bleary eyes as Celia continued to pet his head. 'You'd better move your horse into the barn, Dan. There's men coming as I understand it. We wouldn't want to let them know you're here. Not first thing.'

Dan nodded, but he was slow in responding. He had turned to look down into those eyes, as blue as the mountain skies in April. He could smell, distantly, the scent of jasmine soap and his eyes felt strangely moist.

'I'll see to the black,' he said brusquely. Bending to pick up the Henry repeater and to shuck the revolver from Kyle Handy's holster, he waited while Deucie lifted the bar across the door and went out into the yard again.

He talked to the black horse as he led it to the slab-sided barn where Deucie's little blue roan and the two bay horses apparently belonging to Handy and Celia stood in a row, looking at him. 'I've ridden us into trouble again, that's for sure,' Dan was saying as he unsaddled the black. He paused and looked back toward the house. Tossing his bedroll onto a tool shelf, hanging his supply sack on a rusty nail, he added, 'This time

43

I'm afraid it's a little deeper than usual.'

'*Damn those blue eyes,*' he muttered, but the black horse did not hear, understand or care. Carrying both rifles, Dan returned to the house, looking up and down the tilled valley and upslope to where the trail fed into it. Nothing, no one. Not a sound. So, then, he wondered – where had those earlier-heard shots originated?

Deucie was waiting at the door, standing to one side, half-concealed by the doorframe. Dan noticed her peering eyes, one pale, strong hand and her mouth – lips parted slightly as if she wished to speak but was holding herself back.

The heavy bar was again dropped into place, positioned behind its iron brackets and Dan stood surveying the room. Handy had been helped on to the old russet-colored sofa. Celia was beside him, holding a damp cloth to his head. The old woman had resumed her rocking, intently studying the fireplace where no log burned. Perhaps she was imagining curling gold and crimson flames, the soft crackling of pine logs being consumed. Perhaps she was far distant, hunting some lost dream.

'Did you see anyone out there?' Celia asked anxiously.

'I cut their sign earlier,' Dan replied, leaning

both rifles against the wall in the corner nearest him before seating himself in the matching over-stuffed chair. Deucie stood uncertainly to one side, hands clasped in front of her. Dan some-how managed to keep his eyes off her. 'Two men. Hired by your father.'

'I knew it,' Handy said miserably. His eyes lifted to meet Featherskill's. 'I'm sorry. We didn't know who Amos would hire. Celia thought it would be you, but Deucie said you wouldn't take such a job,'

'Deucie's right,' Dan said with a quick smile. 'He offered me the job: I refused. He found two other men.'

'Do you know them?' Handy asked, sitting up straighter.

'I know them by reputation, and on sight now: Dallas French and Brad Feeley.'

Celia searched Kyle's face intently for intelli-gence. She was squeezing his hand with both of her own. 'Do you know them, Kyle?'

'I've heard the names.' He frowned as if debating whether to share his knowledge with Celia. 'Feeley is supposed to be a conscienceless killer. Dallas French is reputed to be one of the fastest stand-up gunfighters in the territory.' Celia took in a sharp breath and simultaneously let a little moan escape her lips. One thing was obvious to Featherskill – whatever means of inducement Kyle Handy had used to draw the girl away from her home and into the mountains with him, it hadn't been brute force. She sat as near to him as humanly possible, still clinging to his hand, her worshipful eyes on his.

'We've got to get moving, then,' Celia said.

'You're probably safer here,' Featherskill responded, and Kyle Handy nodded in agreement.

'Don't you see, they would have us trapped in here,' Celia said, spreading expressive hands. 'Two men could keep us pinned down forever!'

'Five,' Dan amended.

'What do you mean?' Celia asked.

'There are at least five men on their way up here,' Featherskill had to tell her.

'But who. . . ?' Kyle Handy asked in bewilderment.

'I don't know,' Dan admitted. 'Your father, Celia, hired two of them, French and Feeley. They're supposed to find you and take you back.'

'I'll never go!' the girl said in a flash of anger.

Featherskill ignored the outburst. 'I have no idea who the other three men are or what they're after. Maybe they're in with French and Feeley; maybe your father hired extra protection. Maybe they just want to wait until the first two have done the job and then snatch Celia, grabbing the reward for themselves.'

'I don't get it,' Kyle said, shaking his head heavily. 'But it's making me wonder if maybe we shouldn't do as Celia suggests, get out of here, ride into the high country to hide. If they surround the house, we can't fight our way out.' He was silent and thoughtful for a moment before raising his eyes again to Featherskill's.

'What I don't understand, Featherskill,' Handy said, 'is where you fit in? Are you sure you didn't change your mind about the reward after thinking it over?'

'Dan would never!' Deucie said, speaking for the first time in a while. 'Besides,' she said, a little triumphantly, 'if that was what he had in mind, he'd already be on his way back down the south trail with Celia in tow.'

'That's true, I suppose,' Handy agreed reluctantly.

'I'm here,' Dan said without hesitation, 'for Deucie's sake.' He avoided her glance and continued, 'As for you two, I don't care what you do or where you're going. I'm convinced that

47

Kyle didn't kidnap you, Celia. That being so, you've the right to do whatever you wish.'

'Dan?' Deucie said, taking a step nearer so that he could again detect that faint jasmine scent. 'I don't see how we can fort up here – there won't be any help coming from town, or anywhere. Ever. Not Marshal Highslip. . . ?' It was a hesitant, hopeful question.

'No,' Dan had to tell her. 'I don't hold it against John; he's made it clear he won't be riding up here to help.'

'He sent you?' Celia asked, her voice rising nervously. 'Is that it?'

'In a way. I told you, I came because Deucie was in danger.'

'*Is* in danger!' Celia insisted. 'So are we all – you included. So what are we to do, Mr Featherskill?' her question contained a verbal sneer. 'You're the great warrior. Do we leave or stay?'

'It's not up to him,' Kyle Handy said. But it was bravado; he looked to Featherskill for the answer.

'We can't leave Roxie,' Deucie Campbell said, nodding toward the old woman in the rocker. Roxanne babbled on silently, staring at the fireplace. 'She can't even feed herself or stoke a fire.'

48

'Can't take her; can't leave her,' Handy said.

'Oh, she'll be all right!' Celia said, causing Featherskill's eyebrow to lift slightly. This was her own aunt she was talking about, after all. Logically the girl was right. No one would have cause to harm Roxie, and if they were to build a fire for her, leave food out that she could reach, she would manage well enough until this business could be settled.

'We might never be able to return,' Deucie said quietly, pointing out the flaw in the argument.

'After we're gone you'll be all right, Deucie. You and the old woman,' Handy believed. He had gotten to his feet and with Featherskill's nodded agreement, had picked up his rifle. Dan gave him the pistol from behind his belt. Handy checked the loads and put it back in his holster. 'Featherskill knows this mountain. He can guide us out of here. Then we'll be shut of French and Feeley and you'll be finished with us.'

'No,' Dan said firmly. His mouth was pinched into a thin line. 'That makes a hostage out of Deucie. I won't allow it.'

'Well, damnit!' Celia exploded. 'Someone make a decision; we can't stand around all day talking about what we're going to do.'

'Dan?' Deucie touched his sleeve, and the slight brush of her fingers sent electricity along his spine. 'Look.'

Roxanne was moving her hands in agitated motion, rocking vigorously on her chair. 'What does she want?' Dan asked.

'She's telling us to scram, to get out of here,' Deucie answered.

'She doesn't want to risk being shot, or having her house burned to the ground,' Celia said callously.

'Someone's out there!' Kyle Handy said in a hoarse whisper. He had been peering out the window and now he told them, 'I caught a glimpse of a man in the pines across the field. I'm sure of it.'

Roxanne continued to wave them away with her flailing hands. Celia was in red-faced fury. Handy had his Winchester raised nervously.

Featherskill said, 'Let's saddle the ponies. We're riding.'

The dash to the stable was made in increments. As Kyle covered them from the open window, Dan and Deucie sprinted toward the building. Reaching the open door, Dan nudged Deucie inside while he went to a knee with his rifle and covered the retreat of Celia and Kyle Handy. There were no shots from the pine forest, and strain his eyes as he might, Featherskill did not catch sight of a lurking sniper. He wondered briefly, uselessly, if Handy had been lying about seeing a rider.

Now Dan hurriedly saddled the black as Handy, his bay ready to ride, watched from the doorway. He retied his bedroll and bag of provisions behind the saddle, glad that he had at least had the sense to purchase a few supplies. Deucie stood beside her pretty little blue roan, stroking the horse's muzzle. Her eyes were fixed on Dan's strong hands, on his face, set in concentration as he worked, but they slid quickly away when he had tightened the second cinch and turned toward her.

Unsmiling, Dan nodded to her and they walked the horses to the door. Celia followed, leading Kyle Handy's army bay as well. Dan was suspicious about the origin of those horses, but he said nothing.

The army required their horses to be as uniform as possible. Officers could provide their own mounts, but enlisted men were mounted on bays when possible, by regulation. And one of these horses – Celia's – showed signs of not so long past having been a shavetail – that is, the army bobbed the tails on new horses for cleanliness when they were purchased, hence 'shavetail' for a new officer. Celia's horse's tail had only about half its normal length. All of that flitted rapidly through Dan's mind without conscious thought. He was concerned now with escape.

If there was a man in the pines beyond the field, that meant there was another one somewhere. French and Feeley rode as a team. Were they then both in the pines to the west? Or was one possibly on the wooded crescent-shaped rise behind the house? At any rate, a man under cover was the equal of six in the open and they had to cross that open stubble field to reach the pass leading across Shadow Mountain to the western slope and freedom.

Roughly, Dan told Deucie, 'Stay as far from me as possible. I'll be a target.'

Deucie nodded meekly. There was a hurt look in her eyes and now Dan realized that the way he had phrased the order she might have been upset by the ambiguity of his first sentence. He had said something like that to her under different circumstances not so long ago.

Cursing under his breath, Dan shoved that

thought from his mind as well. 'Let's go, Handy. Fan out as if we're in a picket line. At the first shot, ride like hell for the pines.'

FOUR

At the first shot, Dallas French felt the shock of pain in his left shoulder. His pinto horse reared up and, still pawing for his holstered Colt, Dallas hit the rough ground hard. Scrambling to his feet he dashed toward the shelter of the pines which were thick along the slope. Behind him he heard more shots and he had looked back in time to see the bullet rip into Brad Feeley's skull, killing the dark man instantly.

Now on foot, bleeding badly from his dangling left arm, Dallas wove his way through the tall pines. Behind him the three hunters stretched their horses out into a run to close the distance between them. *Who the hell were they?*

Dallas staggered on through the forest, his shoulder filled with searing pain. He paused once, perspiring heavily, blond hair hanging in his eyes, and tried to bind the shoulder one-handed, using his bandanna. It was a futile experiment and, as the riders continued to approach, he gave it up and ran on, his left hand stuffed into his waist band to keep the dangling arm from swinging.

The clouds which had been hanging low all morning now seemed to scud off the very tips of the pines. The world was dark and damp. Tree trunks loomed up like black pillars. The horse-men still came. There was no outrunning them although the horses had to be slowed to pass through the timber. Dallas's lungs burned, his legs were trembling with the loss of blood. He slid down a small declivity, climbed back up through the bed of strewn pine needles and waited for the approaching men, his Colt cocked and ready in his right hand.

Who were they? A posse? Featherskill and some friends? he wondered.

It was more likely that these three – whoever they were – had heard about the reward, found that he and Feeley had already accepted the job and set out to eliminate them and catch up with the Corbett girl and her man themselves, claim-ing the reward.

In that case, Dallas considered, why hadn't they let Feeley and himself take the risks, do the work for them and then ambush them on their return? It made no sense. Neither did it matter; all that mattered now was staying alive. He could still see the stunned, dead look in Feeley's eyes, eyes that were no longer connected to his brain.

Dallas waited. Cold moisture soaked his shirt, trickled down his spine. The mist was low enough to touch the ground. Visibility was almost nil. Dallas kept his ear pressed to the ground. He would hear the horses before he saw them.

But abruptly there was a voice so near the man seemed to be standing next to him. Clenching his revolver's grip even more tightly, Dallas looked up, but he saw no one.

The voice said, 'The hell with this. We're wasting time!'

Then there was utter silence. Dallas lay shivering in the damp and cold, the life trickling out of him. He neither saw nor heard the riders depart; they were silent spirits in the gloom of the forest. After a long half-hour during which he grew colder yet and his limbs stiffened, Dallas French rose and climbed on to the flat ground above him.

He stood with his arm dangling, Colt clenched in the other, searching the gray day and dark woods around him, his blue shirt pasted to his body by dampness. His eyes were narrow and hard. The gunman sheltered a cold fury in his mind.

They had ambushed them. Killed Brad Freeley – not that Brad amounted to much, but he was French's partner. These three men were snatching money from his pocket by pursuing the Corbett girl. Worst of all they had disrespected him.

Anyone who knew Dallas would have made damn sure he was dead after dry-gulching him. Anyone who knew the quick-handed Trinidad gunfighter would have known that only wounding him would mean looking over your shoulder for the trailing wolf the rest of your life. These men were apparently too stupid to know that: they would learn.

Dallas straggled on through the woods, pausing now and then to lean a hand against a pine to catch his breath. Water dripped from their high reaches. The ground was growing sodden underfoot. His heart was hammering, his head thudded with dull pain. No matter. He walked on, forcing his body to obey the mastery of his growing hatred.

He had no idea where his pinto had gotten to. He knew where Brad Feeley's sorrel was, if the three ambushers hadn't taken it. And if it too was gone – no matter.

If he had to, he would follow them on bloody stumps until he had unleashed his vengeance on the three cowards.

When the shots came, they seemed distant. There were many of them, but Featherskill saw no gunmen, saw no smoke rising from the pines. Nevertheless he followed his own command as the others had done, and heeled the black horse sharply, racing it toward the cover of the mist-shrouded pines beyond the stubble field.

He kept his eye on Deucie as she galloped her blue roan along. The roan moved in brisk, light movements; Deucie was an easy rider, deft with her touch. One more thing he had always admired about the woman. He reined up beside her among the huge pines and turned the black's head back toward the valley. No one was following. No one rushed toward them from the forest depths, guns blazing.

'Whoever that is, they weren't shooting at us,' Dan said.

'Then who. . . ?' Deucie asked.

'I don't know. Let's not waste time trying to figure it out. Let's keep traveling while we can.'

Kyle had walked his horse up beside them. Overhearing Dan's words, Kyle was in quick agreement.

'I'm with you. Let's keep it moving.' He and Celia started on immediately although neither of them knew the way west. Deucie hesitated, her horse side-stepping with nervous eagerness. Her wide blue eyes were on the house across the valley.

'Roxie will be all right,' Dan said, reading Deucie's thoughts.

'She's so old, Dan,' Deucie replied in a concerned whisper. 'How will she ever take care of herself?'

'We'll be back before nightfall,' Dan promised, with no real hope of accomplishing that feat. Deucie lifted hopeful eyes to him.

'I know we won't, Dan.' They started their horses on through the pine and cedar forest. Occasionally now there were pockets of aspen. There were many on the higher slopes of Shadow Mountain when they could be glimpsed through a rent in the shifting clouds. The wind had increased. It whined through the trees, swaying them. Pine cones fell like hail. The clouds were now thicker, heavier and the air was growing cold.

'Lucky if we don't get snow,' Dan commented, pulling up the collar of his buffalo coat.

Deucie looked skyward and nodded. Her thoughts were still on the old woman in the cabin. 'It hasn't been an easy life for Roxanne,' she commented, as they rode on side by side. She ducked an overhanging branch, flipped her head so that her heavy yellow braid went back across her shoulder and told him, 'When Dad brought Roxanne home I was happy for him. He hadn't been himself since Mother died. Roxanne still had a lingering beauty about her. She used to be an actress, they said. Well, you saw her back then.'

'Only a few times.' Dan had faint memories of a tall, square-shouldered, red-haired woman with a false smile. 'She didn't leave the house much.'

'And you didn't come in much,' Deucie said with a small smile. 'Roxie didn't like the wilderness life, of course. I suppose she thought Dad had a big landholding—'

'Which he did.'

Deucie waved a hand. 'Not like this, Dan. She

was from the south. Maybe she thought with a thousand acres Dad had a huge plantation. Well, as we know, only about twenty acres of land is really arable . . . marginally.'

Dan kept his eye on Kyle Handy and Celia, riding fifty feet or so ahead of them. Their heads were together, speaking in low voices. Young lovers, what could you expect? Only they didn't quite act like young lovers. What Dan sensed about them was indefinite but troubling. Deucie was still talking.

'After Dad passed away, after he was no longer there to encourage Roxie to garden or ride with him, she almost never came out of the house. She sat and watched the fire.'

'Lost youth, lost dreams?' Dan suggested.

'I suppose so,' Deucie said with a faint sigh. 'She's only a shell now, but Dan, she's still my stepmother. I am concerned about her.'

Deucie would be concerned about any human being left behind. Dan knew that much about her. He only nodded, however; he had no mean-ingful advice to offer. Kyle Handy and Celia had halted ahead of them, their horses circling, pawing at the earth. They were lost, Dan thought, with a shameless grin.

'I thought if I could see the peak, I could find

my way,' Handy said. He took off his hat and shook the water off it. 'Damn this fog!'

'Landmarks wouldn't help much unless you've been this way before,' Dan told Handy. 'We've got to climb higher – it's going to get a little rougher, but we have to. Straight ahead a mile or so is a gorge; there's no crossing, so we angle north. It's five miles or so to trailhead.'

'Well, let's do what we have to do,' Celia said impatiently. She wore that almost-angry little pout of hers. Was it true anger or just nerves?

'I think we should rest the horses,' Kyle said, 'if the trail is going to be as rough as Featherskill says. Look, there's no one behind us, and we will need to keep the horses fresh.'

It was not a bad suggestion, but Dan wondered why it had occurred now to Kyle. The man had been all for urgent flight. Now he seemed in no particular hurry to reach the Shadow Mountain's western slopes. But since they had heard the gunfire back there Handy's demeanor had changed. Or so it seemed. Dan decided that he was doing altogether too much useless pondering these days.

'All right,' Dan agreed. 'Loosen up your cinches and we'll let them breathe awhile.'

Alone beside Deucie as she eased the cinches

on her blue roan, he asked quietly, 'Did you have time to snatch up a gun when we left the house, Deucie?'

She looked at him curiously. For an answer, she swept back the skirt of her lambskin coat and showed him the holstered Remington .36 riding her hip. Concern drew her fair eyebrows together.

'Why?'

'I think we may have trouble here, Deucie.'

She laughed. 'You think so? Just because we have some hired guns up here trying to kidnap my cousin and kill Kyle – and probably anyone who tries to get in their way.'

Featherskill had to smile in return. 'What I mean is there's something going on here that I don't understand. Remember those gunshots?' he asked. 'Who was that?' He went on to explain some of his conjectures, but they were hardly illuminating.

In the end all Deucie could do was shrug her small shoulders and say, 'If you've got a bad feeling about things, I'll stay alert.'

'Please.' Hesitantly he added, 'I can't have anything happen to you, Deucie.' But he could not look at her when he said that and returned to fiddling unnecessarily with his saddle cinches.

And since he wasn't looking at her he couldn't see Deucie smiling gently at him behind his back.

They walked to where Celia and Kyle Handy stood, apparently deep in dispute. Overhead the tips of the pines swayed heavily in the increasing wind, and there was a still coldness settling ominously over the deep forest. It would snow, soon and hard, Featherskill decided. They would have to get going and soon if they were going to reach the western trail. If they could achieve that before the bounty hunters found them, the snow could work very well to their advantage, covering their tracks.

Celia was saying, 'We have to keep moving, Kyle! Those are killers back there.'

'We need fresh horses under us,' Handy said without calming her.

'I *am not* going back to the ranch, Kyle. And I will not have you killed. That is not love, to let you risk such a fate.' She nodded toward the standing bays. 'The horses look rested enough to me. What do you say, Dan?'

'It's time we were riding,' Featherskill answered. He didn't want to get involved in their argument, but he had to worry about Celia's hide and Deucie's as well. Too bad if the horses grew weary; under these circumstances they would have to be pushed.

Kyle persisted, 'By the time they catch up, their horses will be beat! We'll have four animals ready to run.' His expression was pleading. 'Don't any of you see my point?'

'We all do,' Deucie answered. 'The thing is, we don't know how far behind they are, and our ponies have had a chance to blow.'

'You see!' Celia said with a note of frustrated triumph in her voice. 'We all agree. Kyle, we have to ride!'

'You all feel that way?' Kyle Handy asked, his blue eyes going from face to face. With a shrug he nodded and drew his Colt revolver. 'Well, then, we'll have it this way. I didn't mean to have this happen so soon, but you've forced it. Put your hands up, all of you!' he commanded, as he thumbed back the hammer on his revolver.

'Kyle!' Celia rushed at him, her eyes wild. He shoved her away. She spun around and found herself roughly seated on the ground. 'Are you crazy?'

'He's not crazy,' Dan said. 'Just showing his true colors. He's with the men following us – aren't you, Kyle?'

'Shut up. Unbuckle your gun and stand away from your horse. I'll be having your rifle too.'

'What is going on here?' Celia shrieked, rising from the ground. Her hair was in her face and she brushed it away. 'We're running away . . . like you wanted, Kyle. I thought we were going to be married.' Her lower lip trembled as she spoke these last words.

'Oh, we will be, Celia, you can be sure of that,' he answered. 'Kick that gunbelt away, Featherskill, and step away from it!'

'Celia—' Deucie held out her arms to her cousin. At the same time she gave Dan a little sidelong glance, indicating the holstered Remington she carried, concealed beneath her coat flap. He shook his head. No, not now. There was no chance of beating Kyle Handy while standing in his gun sights.

'What's happening!' Celia moaned. She went into Deucie's arms and Deucie stroked her head.

'I'm afraid Kyle is a devious man,' Deucie replied. 'He wants you because he wants Corbett's ranch. Isn't that right, Handy?'

'You're a smart lady, aren't you?' Handy asked. His demeanor had changed dramatically. His eyes were no longer boyish, but hard, his mouth slightly cruel.

'I don't understand . . . our plans.' Celia was nearly incoherent. Featherskill picked up

Deucie's thread of logic.

'If he marries you, he's married to the owner of the Corbett Ranch. Isn't that right, Handy? I'll bet that your mother, Susan, never made a will including her second husband, Amos Corbett. The land, the cattle, the buildings – all of it – most likely goes to you, Celia. Amos knows that. I don't know how Kyle knew.'

'County recorder's office. I've been looking for a way to get my start, Featherskill. Marrying money seems to be the easiest way there is. Corbett would have stopped it, of course, if he could. He's as greedy as anybody. After all, his idea in marrying Susan in the first place was to get his hands on the ranch, wasn't it?'

'I wouldn't know,' Featherskill replied, but he suspected Kyle Handy was right.

'I won't marry you now!' Celia said, spinning to face him. 'Not ever!'

Kyle Handy's voice was very cold as he answered, 'Oh, yes, you will, Celia. If you want to keep on living as you have been.' He added cruelly, 'If you want to keep on living.'

'What does he mean, Dan?' Deucie asked. She was shivering with the cold now and the chill of the moment. She moved nearer to Dan, easing the pistol closer, but Kyle Handy followed her with the muzzle of his Colt.

'He means that if Celia doesn't consent, he'll find another woman to stand in for her. In another state, who would know? Everyone back home knows that Celia ran off with Kyle. They'll assume they were married. Then Celia will have a terrible accident of some kind—'

'No!' Celia shrieked. She started to rush at Kyle again, her small fists held high, but she halted, knowing the man would simply club her down again. 'It can't be.'

'You're too damn smart, Featherskill,' Kyle Handy said. 'That's why we wanted you out of this to begin with. When you turned old Amos down on his job offer, I thought we had it made. I didn't count on you still being sweet on Deucie. I asked around. The last I heard you two weren't even on speaking terms. My mistake.'

'You covered for it,' Dan said. Deucie glanced at Dan for an explanation. He told her, 'He hired three men for protection. Probably they're to get a share of the ranch or some cash money – there will be a lot of money coming in after round-up, after those cattle are sold.'

'I still don't understand,' Deucie said.

'Amos Corbett hired two bounty hunters to come after Handy and Celia,' Dan answered,

'Brad Feeley and Dallas French. Handy couldn't do anything about that. What he could do was hire some thugs of his own. Three other men. That's why he's not worried about the bounty hunters.'

Featherskill went on as the sky darkened and the first snowflakes began to fall through the forest, 'These three managed to get ahead of French and Feeley. They probably ambushed them.'

'How could they do that?'

'Simple. Celia knew where the South Pass trail was. She showed Kyle. He then marked it for his three hired guns. They were on Shadow Mountain first, laying an ambush for Feeley and French who rode the slope trail. Remember those shots we heard? That was what they were. An ambush.

'Now he's waiting for those three to join us. Isn't that about it, Handy?'

'That's about it,' Kyle Handy said slowly. 'They'll catch up soon enough. But I'm not waiting for them to take care of things.'

'Meaning?' Dan asked carefully, as Handy took a step nearer.

'You're the joker in the deck, Featherskill. I can't have you showing up on the table again. I could take you prisoner, but I'd rather have you dead.' Handy's finger tightened on the trigger and the gun exploded with deadly accuracy, sending Dan Featherskill tumbling back to fall heavily, his face slamming into the cold forest earth, the sounds of a woman's scream in his ears.

FIVE

As Kyle Handy triggered off his Colt, several things happened at once. Celia screamed and launched herself at Kyle's gun arm, too late to stop the first bullet, but effective in keeping Kyle from firing again immediately. The black horse reared up in surprise and Deucie leaped toward Featherskill, her eyes wide with terror. And the .44 slug from the muzzle of Kyle Handy's revolver tore through Featherskill's buffalo coat and ripped a deep gash along his side.

'Stop it!' Dan heard Celia scream. He saw Deucie's face above him, a brief blur, and then she backed away quickly as the black horse, startled into motion, leaped between them. Instinct caused Dan to reach out and grab the stirrup of his saddle. He shouted to the black, encouraging

71

it to run. Confused though it might have been, the black knew his master's command and lowered his head to charge off through the pines, Dan clinging to the stirrup.

Dan's arm felt as if it would jerk from his shoulder socket; there was hot blood leaking across his belly. The horse dragged him over rocks, tree roots and through thorny clumps of brush, but Kyle's following shots, fired wildly into the forest, came nowhere near him.

A quarter of a mile on, Dan's grip failed him and he fell free, half-rolling to the base of a massive pine tree. He tried to get to his knees, reached automatically for his missing pistol and then, shaking his head like a dog, he dragged himself behind the pine.

The black, confused but having run off its first burst of panic, had halted and stood, reins trailing, not thirty feet away. It was a long thirty feet. On hands and knees, Dan scooted that way, hearing the rush of hoofbeats behind him somewhere, a shout without intelligible words. Dan reached the black which stood patiently, if in annoyance at these human games, and dragged himself upright using the stirrup. Finally, securing a grip on the pommel he pulled himself into the saddle, reaching below the horse's neck to gather up the dangling reins.

He paused, hair in his eyes, side bleeding freely, took a slow painful breath and then kneed the black, walking it through the forest rather than letting it break into flight. Dan rode a circuitous path, weaving through the heavy pines, eyes constantly alert although his vision was growing blurry. He paused frequently to listen, but now he heard no pursuing hoofbeats and he figured that Kyle had given up his mad chase. He would know that he had no chance of catching Dan now, except by chance. He knew he had nothing more to fear from the unarmed Dan Featherskill. Not against Handy himself and three additional armed men.

Dan recognized this as well and he breathed many bitter curses. Sliding from the saddle he propped himself up against the bole of a huge tree and unbuttoned his coat. Yanking up his black shirt he saw the ugly wound there. Wiping the drying blood from it, he was grateful to find that the deep groove had missed all organs, all bone. That did not stop it from bleeding copiously and hurting like hell.

Dan took his skinning knife from its boot sheath and slit his shirttails with its thin, razor-edged blade. Then he ripped two long strips from the bottom of it. Moving uncomfortably he leaned forward and, twisting painfully, managed to bind the wound superficially.

He wanted to sleep then. The loss of blood had brought a heavy weariness. He leaned back against the tree, staring skyward. The snow caused him to return to his senses and rise from the ground. It was going to snow hard. Pretty twisting clusters of white flakes dropped through the high branches of the pines and settled to earth. Soon, if the roar of thunder and rush of wind could be used as a gauge, those flakes would be a heavy, frozen wash of snow.

There was snow melting on the black's back and in its mane as Dan again fought his way aboard, his head reeling as he sat there, trying to formulate a plan. He did not like his chances, not at all. Maybe, he thought hopefully, there was a chance of catching up with Handy before he was joined by his three hired guns. The odds were terrible, Dan thought, even as he unbuckled his saddle-bag and removed his spare Colt revolver, unwrapping the protective oilskin. He loaded it from one of the boxes of extra ammunition he had stashed there. He looked at the gun he held, knowing what deadly force it contained, knowing also that it would be of little use if he were forced to stand and fight four men armed not only with revolvers, but long guns as well.

It did not matter what the odds were: Deucie must be saved! Now, she too knew of Kyle Handy's scheme, of the murders that had likely already occurred on the mountain in its execution. Would Handy hesitate to kill her? Not likely. He had already spoken of 'getting rid' of Celia if she didn't agree to the plan, and Featherskill doubted he meant putting her away in a nunnery.

The snow continued to fall. His body continued to leak hot blood. There was nothing ahead of him but wilderness and blizzard, nothing behind but the outlaw guns. The trees swayed and creaked in the strengthening wind, the sky went dark and the land grew bitterly cold.

Featherskill turned the black horse's head and started slowly, slowly back toward the farmhouse through the havoc of the settling storm.

Deucie put yet another seasoned pine log on the fire, crouching before the hearth to jab at the embers with the black iron poker. Kyle Handy sat on the divan, far across the room, his coat thrown on the floor. Celia sat near him, her eyes downcast miserably, her hand clasped between her knees. Roxanne sat in her rocking chair, utterly still now. She might have been a lifeless image except for the firelight dancing in her eyes, the slow working of her jaw.

'Get away from that fire now,' Kyle commanded Deucie. 'And be careful what you do with that poker.'

Obediently she replaced the hooked poker on its stand and eased away from the fire. She still had her coat buttoned, concealing the holstered pistol she carried, but Kyle seemed to have taken no notice of this incongruity.

'I don't see how you plan on going anywhere,' Deucie said. She had eased along the log wall to lean against it, as distant from Handy as she could position herself. She nodded toward the window. 'This storm is going to settle in good and proper. When it snows up here, the passes are all blocked.'

'Shut up,' was Kyle Handy's answer. 'Do you see anybody coming out there?'

Deucie glanced out the fogged window toward the fields which were already covered eight inches deep by a blanket of snow.

'No one.'

'They'll be here,' he said mostly to himself.

'If they don't know this country,' Deucie said,

'traveling through the snowstorm could—'

'Shut up,' Kyle said again, angrily. 'I don't need your advice, don't want to hear your chatter. They aren't stupid. They can follow the smoke on the wind. They'll be here.'

'What are we going to do then, Kyle?' Celia asked, lifting her unhappy gaze from the threadbare carpet.

'Get off this damned mountain before we *are* snowed in. Find us a preacher or justice of the peace.'

'I told you that I won't—'

'I told you that you will!' Kyle growled. He yanked her head back by the hair and looked into her eyes with dangerous meaning. 'I have come too far. We are going through with the plan.'

'All for the ranch?' Celia shouted, twisting free of his grip. 'Kyle, I loved you. The ranch would have been ours anyway!'

'When? When old Amos dies? He wouldn't let go of that land without a fight, and you know it. He'd have had me killed. That's what he was trying anyway, isn't it?' Celia nodded meekly. 'He would have continued to rake in the profits. Maybe he would have let me work as a cattle hand. He's not a generous man, Celia.

'Besides,' he said, leaning back, his voice lowering to a mocking tone, 'I don't intend for the ranch to be *our* place. It'll be mine, Celia. In fact and in name. I couldn't live being beholden to you. Saying "Yes, darling, yes sweetheart, whatever you say", hating you for making a dog of me for fear I'd get kicked out on my ear.'

'I would never have—!' Celia protested, but Kyle didn't seem to hear her.

'I've seen those situations before. I'd never let it happen to me. I am a *man*, Celia! Do you understand that?'

'Yes,' she murmured, her lips barely moving.

'I'll have it all. And legally. If Amos Corbett tries to get nasty about it – well, I've got three good gunhands with me. He's only got a kid, an old man with a wooden leg and that Mexican cook on the place. I know that: I checked it out. Everyone else is out on round-up. How's he going to fight the four of us? This was the time to act. When those cattle are sold, the cash money will come flowing in. To me, Celia. Not to Amos Corbett. To me. I had this all well planned out ahead of time, you see. I was waiting.'

'And buttering Celia up,' Deucie said. Kyle's malevolent eyes flickered toward her.

'It didn't take much. She couldn't stand Amos

either, could you, Celia? Couldn't stand living with the self-important old leech any longer.'

'I thought—' Celia began. Deucie's words interrupted her remark.

'I see a rider,' Deucie said, looking out the window. She wiped the fogged pane clean. Snowflakes adhered to the glass and slid away. Her heart had risen at first. She had hoped, prayed that somehow Dan had escaped, that he had returned. Now her heart sank. 'There's three of them. It's your hired guns, Kyle.'

All of them were startled by the sudden loud screech and thump. Roxanne Campbell had slid from her chair, trying to rise to make her way to the window. Deucie gave a surprised little shriek and went to her.

'Roxie,' she admonished, helping up her fragile stepmother, 'you can't be doing that, and you know it. Is there something you want? I'll get it for you.' She eased Roxanne back onto her chair and covered her birdlike shoulders with her shawl.

'I thought she was a cripple,' Kyle said.

'What do you call this!' Deucie said angrily. Then she gently stroked Roxie's thin gray hair, brushing it from her sunken eyes. Kyle wasn't interested enough to continue the conversation.

He was on his feet, the front door flung open. Snow drifted in, blown from the heavy, shifting curtains of the storm. Handy was waving to the dark figures of the approaching horsemen.

'Over here!' Then he stepped out onto the porch, the cold wind gusting through the house, beating down the fire. 'The shed, Marsh!' they heard him call through cupped hands. 'Put your horses up over there!'

Then he came in, closing the plank door behind him. He was grinning with dark satisfaction. His eyes when he fixed them on the others were triumphant. 'You see, everything is working out all right. I had it all planned.'

'What about the others?' Celia asked with a flicker of hope. 'The two men Amos hired to find us.'

'They won't be showing up,' Kyle answered with grim satisfaction. 'Not if my men are here.'

'Amos will send more men,' Deucie said, although she didn't believe it herself. She wanted to plant some doubt in the boastful young man's mind.

'Never,' Handy said with a dismissive wave of his hand. 'He's got no money to hire anyone even if he could find more men of that kind. Besides,' Kyle went on, 'there's the snowstorm, isn't there? And we will be long gone ourselves before anybody can hit our backtrail.'

'Where. . . ?' Celia asked weakly.

'That's to be determined. The snow changes things a little. No matter. We will be married in a matter of days. Then Amos won't even have a reason for sending anyone after us, will he?'

'He'll kill you,' Celia said with unexpected venom.

'He's had his try,' Kyle said with bleak confidence. 'Now it's my turn.'

Kyle didn't see Roxanne's eyes flicker at this cold promise to have her brother, Amos, killed. If he had, it's doubtful that he could have guessed at the significance. He was attentive now only to his plan, basking in his own momentary glory. The old woman began rocking again, furiously, her eyes fixed deeply on firelight images.

They heard the heavy thumping of boots on the porch and Kyle flung the door open in welcome. The first man through entered, stamping the snow from his boots, carrying a double-barreled twelve-gauge shotgun. He did not take Kyle's hand, but nodded to him as he walked directly to the hearth.

'Hello, Marsh,' Kyle said expansively. 'How are you?'

'Damned cold,' the thick-shouldered, bearded man muttered. He turned his back to the fire and glowered at the three women. 'Which one's the bride?'

'This is Celia,' Kyle said with a hint of vestigial pride.

'Then who's she?' Marsh wanted to know, leveling a stubby finger at Deucie.

'Her cousin. This is her place. The old lady's her stepmother, Celia's aunt.'

'Not Corbett's sister!' Marsh asked with a booming laugh. 'Well, what do you know? Did you hear that, Bedel?'

The lanky gunfighter with the thin red beard answered in a low, irritated voice, 'I don't care who she is. I want to know what the plan is.' He nodded toward the window, at the swirling blizzard beyond. 'We got to get off this mountain.'

'Late in the year for snow, ain't it?' the youngest of the three, a prematurely balding ape of a man asked. None of the men paid any attention to him.

'It's different in the high country,' Deucie responded. 'We often get one or two of these in the high country even when it's already round-up time in the valley.'

'Something you didn't consider, Handy,'

Marsh scolded. Kyle didn't like his tone, that was obvious. He, after all, was the one who had hired these three. He was the boss. But he did not answer the recrimination.

'We're leaving,' he said easily. 'Back down the South Pass to the western slopes. No one will be up and about in this weather. Once we hit the flats, we head south for Carver Springs. They've got a justice of the peace there.'

'When do we get paid?' the balding man asked.

'Where you going to spend it, Jeremy?' Bedel asked mockingly.

'We'll get ours, don't worry,' Marsh said, stroking his beard. He was beginning to make Kyle uneasy.

'First of all,' Kyle Handy asked, 'are you sure there's nobody on our backtrail?'

Marsh said, 'Do you mean, did we take care of those two gunnies Corbett hired? The answer is yes.'

'I took one of 'em out of the saddle with a head-shot,' Jeremy said with obvious satisfaction. 'But, Marsh, the other one he—'

'Shut up!' Marsh said angrily.

Kyle looked worried again. 'The other one *what?*' he demanded.

'The other one got winged in the shoulder,' Bedel said. 'Knocked to the ground, but he got up and ran on us. Couldn't find him in this weather.'

'What do you suppose he's going to do!' Marsh asked in a thunderous voice. 'He was bleeding like a stuck hog. You saw the blood. Is he going to run us down on foot? In this blizzard?'

'Who was it?' Kyle asked a little shakily.

'Blond-haired man. I don't know his name.'

'*Dallas French*,' Kyle provided. 'Damnit all!'

'French?' Jeremy asked, rubbing his balding head vigorously as if to facilitate thought. 'Isn't he that fast-draw artist from Trinidad?'

'That's him,' Kyle said. 'He was the one I was worried about when word got around that he was in town.'

'He's got a reputation,' Bedel said.

Marsh moved into the center of the floor, dominating the room. Angrily he said, 'The man is half-dead, afoot in a snowstorm. I don't care who he is – a reputation doesn't make a man unkillable. Which brings to mind, Handy, what happened to Featherskill? Did you manage to take care of him?'

'I got him. Shot him out in the pines.'

'But you didn't kill him,' Deucie said softly, and the men turned in unison to stare at the small blonde girl. Marsh began to grow angry again.

'You had the drop on him and you didn't kill him!'

'His horse got in the way,' Handy said feebly. 'You weren't there.'

'No! I wasn't there, or he'd damn sure be dead.' He took a deep breath and said with a show of confidence, 'No matter, His reputation don't count for much, no more than Dallas French's. We've got the numbers, the horses and our hostages.' He nodded at Celia and Deucie. '*She*,' he said, meaning Deucie Campbell, 'rides with us, too. Just in case we have to negotiate with Featherskill or his ghost.'

'We'd better move soon,' Jeremy said worriedly.

'Start getting the horses ready. You and Bedel both. I'll see what kind of grub we can grab out of the pantry here. Then we ride.'

'Which way?'

'South Pass like you said. It's the only way, isn't it? Dallas French is up to the north, if he did manage to survive somehow, Featherskill over to the west. We take that rugged trail and they'll have no chance at trying an ambush if they are alive.'

'South Pass, now?' Deucie stepped toward the men, looking at Kyle and then settling her blue eyes on Marsh's cruel face. 'You don't know that trail. It's fine when it's dry, but when it rains hard or snows, it's a nightmare. There's no trees to fence the snow, nothing but rock slabs, and so it slides off easy. The trail gets icy, the trail can be blocked by landslides or avalanches – for days at a time. Nobody will come looking for us. No one will know we're there. If we're trapped on that trail, mister . . . we'll die on it.'

Kyle looked anxiously at Marsh. 'If the girl's right, we're in trouble.'

Marsh studied Deucie's blue eyes and then waved her words away. 'She's only thinking of slowing us up, maybe hoping Featherskill is on his way to save her. We came up that trail just like you did. We can ride back down it just as well. It's the only way.'

Kyle nodded mutely. He supposed Marsh was right. They had to ride back down the South Pass trail. Still, even as he put on his buffalo coat and picked up his rifle, Deucie's words echoed in the back of his mind.

If we're trapped on that trail we'll die on it.

SIX

Deucie's dainty little blue roan picked its way
nimbly down the mountain trail as thunder
boomed to the north following a brilliant strike
of forked white lightning. The snow fell heavily
and the land was dark beneath a field of heavy
clouds. The bay horses Celia and Kyle Handy
rode were heavier animals and unused to the
mountains. They moved fearfully, cautiously,
along behind Deucie. She could not see the
three gunmen and she didn't bother to look
back. Her thoughts were fixed on the precipi-
tous trail, the gusting wind and the falling snow.

Where was Dan? Was he even alive? Surely he
was, and he would have caught his horse by now.
She knew, too, that Dan always carried a spare
pistol in his saddle-bags.

The blue roan halted, shook its head and went on only at Deucie's gentle nudging with her knees. There were stones, uptilted slabs of rock underfoot, some of them covered now with snow. Among the heavy clouds, soon it would be difficult to tell the trail from the sheer drop-off to her right. Hitting a patch of ice could send a horse sliding over the rim, Deucie knew.

No one said a word. It would have been almost impossible over the rush of the roaring wind, but rounding a hairpin bend in the trail Deucie could see them following her like silent specters. Ghost riders. Celia now held herself apart from Kyle. She felt betrayed, angry, threatened. As did Deucie. They only needed her to lead the way down the trail and to point them toward Carver Springs where Celia and Kyle were to 'wed'. And they said that they wanted to hold Deucie hostage in case Dan did manage somehow to catch up. How, on this trail under these conditions, was something that could not be guessed. After they were sure they were in the clear, well, they would have no more reason to keep Deucie alive. She would be a witness to their crimes then, and they could afford no witnesses.

Coming to a place where the trail widened beneath an overhanging bluff, Deucie held up her pony for a few minutes – they were getting too strung out along the trail. Watching the men approach, she felt hot anger in her heart. She remembered them talking about Roxie. Deucie had begged them not to leave her stepmother alone in the cabin.

'She can't take care of herself!'

'What're we going to do,' Marsh had asked roughly, 'take her riding down that trail in hard weather?'

'She'll be all right,' Handy had said coldly. She has food here, There's a few logs.'

Marsh added, 'She can get up, too, I saw her do it.'

'You don't understand,' Deucie pleaded. 'She doesn't have enough wood to last out the storm, nor enough food. No one will come this way for days, maybe weeks now. Few people ever pass by anyway.'

'They don't care,' Celia said through clenched teeth. 'They don't care about anybody.' Her eyes raked Kyle Handy's face. He seemed a little unnerved by her hateful glare.

In the end there was nothing they could do for Roxie. Deucie stoked the fire, covered her stepmother's shoulders with her shawl and kissed her dry cheek. 'I'm sorry, Roxie,' she murmured, but the old woman had not answered. Perhaps she was not even there. Perhaps she was off in that flickering dream-fire world of hers.

'What'd you stop for!' Marsh shouted as he drew up beside Deucie on the wide spot on the trail. He had a red woolen scarf wrapped over his head. His eyebrows and beard were heavy with frost.

'You told me not to get too far ahead. You said—'

'Yeah, I said I'd shoot you if you made a break for it. That didn't mean I want you to start dragging your heels. What're you doing, trying to make it easier for Featherskill to catch us?' He lifted his gloved hand and for a moment Deucie thought he was going to strike her, but he slowly lowered his fist and growled. 'Keep moving, girl!'

'How much farther?' Jeremy, the bald little ape asked, his teeth chattering. 'How high up are we.'

'Only about five thousand feet,' Deucie said. 'But the trail switches back a lot. You rode up it, you should remember.'

'When we rode up,' Jeremy said bleakly, 'it didn't look nothing like this.'

The trail was an indistinct hairline winding along the snow-screened slope ahead of them. To their left the sheer wall of shale jutted skyward, the peak of the crest clipped off flat, lost in low clouds. To the right the canyon fell away 5000 feet to a bottom that could not be seen through still more obscuring clouds. The view ahead opened and closed at intervals as the storm drifted on its inexorable fitful journey.

Now the clouds would part and they would see a sun-bright curtain of snow falling ahead of them; then the darkness would return and all was obscured.

'We can't make it down, Marsh!' Jeremy said in anguish. 'Look at that! And the snow's getting deeper on the ground with every minute.'

'Shut up,' Marsh said angrily, though his fury was not directed at Jeremy, but at the weather itself: The snow, hock-deep on the horses already, was continuing to fall, folding down coldly over them. When Marsh kicked away the new snow, he found treacherous ice underneath. 'We've got to keep going,' he said in a voice that was loud but tinged with bitter uncertainty.

Bedel suggested, 'Maybe we could hold up here for a while, Marsh. The bank is cutting the wind. Maybe the snow will stop after a while.'

'Is the storm going to let up, missie?' Marsh asked Deucie and she shook her head slightly. 'Then we've got to push on. Get down before the trail's blocked completely.'

'Bedel's right,' Kyle Handy said. He wore a gray scarf across the bottom of his face, a bandanna held his hat. 'We should wait here for a while. See if it clears. If it doesn't . . . well, we can go back up, shelter up in the cabin.'

'Wait there and see who shows up!' Marsh exploded. 'No thank you.'

Handy was defeated. He nodded his head, 'All right, Marsh. Whatever you say.'

Deucie swept back her coat to have the freedom for mounting and Celia's eyes quickly caught the dull gleam of her cousin's pistol in the dull light. She made a small hissing sound and grabbed Deucie's arm, pulling her aside. The men could not hear her above the whine and rush of the wind.

'Let me have that gun, Deucie.'

'No!' Deucie said, pushing her cousin's hand away.

'I've got to have it, don't you see?' Celia asked. Her teeth chattered as she spoke. Marsh was yelling at them to climb aboard their ponies. 'I can shoot Kyle. With him dead, the game will be up. They'll have no reason to keep on with this plan if he's not around for me to marry! Don't you see, Deucie?'

'And they'll just ride off?'

'Sure,' Celia said, her eyes gleaming brightly. 'What else can they do? There's no profit in them keeping us. Only danger. They'll have to fight if Dan catches up. If they let us go, you'll be free too. Dan won't have a reason to hunt them down. They can ride on down the mountain and we can go back to see to Roxie.'

Her voice lowered to a murderous tone. 'Just give me that pistol, Deucie. I'll shoot his head off where he stands.'

'No.' Deucie hadn't hesitated even a bit. Celia was probably right, but there would be no murder done with her gun – not even of a scheming man like Kyle Handy. If necessary, Deucie would protect herself and her cousin with that Remington, but she would not see murder committed with it. 'You can't have it, Celia. We'll just have to take our chance.'

Celia was rigid with anger. The hostility in her eyes bored into Deucie's. 'No wonder Featherskill wouldn't marry you, Deucie. You're a crazy woman. And a coward as well!'

Deucie pushed Celia away again and swung

93

into the saddle. Marsh had eased his horse nearer, his black eyes savage. 'What the hell are you two doing! We've got to get down that trail *now*. It's only going to get worse.' Having said that he slapped Deucie's roan on the rump and the little horse, startled by the blow, stutter-stepped ahead a little, its small hoofs slipping on the ice beneath the snow.

Deucie controlled the blue roan with pats, soft words and a gentle urging and started on through the falling darkness and swirl of snow toward the depths of the canyon.

Her eyes stung with hot tears which soon became small icy tracks down her cheeks. She bit bitterly at her lower lip as she rode cautiously down the treacherous trail. She felt the urge to shout a defense at Celia, even knowing that her cousin had only said what she had out of hateful spite.

'Dan knows I am not crazy, Celia,' Deucie said to herself. 'And he knows I'm not a coward.' The real reason was much simpler, and too common. Dan was a wandering man, and a warrior. To expect him to settle down was only wishful think-ing on her part. They had argued – it had been a bitter argument, Deucie telling him that he was doomed to die on his wild adventures, leaving her a widow before she had a chance to be a real wife. Dan had looked into her eyes and told her flatly that he was not meant to settle down, that there was a wild and free land out there and that he was not born to be a farmer.

To prove his point he had ridden off with Bo Buckley, joined up to fight in that Sweetwater River range war and stayed away for an entire year. Proving Deucie's point, Buckley got himself killed in the fracas.

Anyway, it was none of Celia's business. Her new-found savagery was worrisome. Deucie had no doubt that her cousin would have carried out her plot to kill Kyle out of hand if she had gotten hold of the pistol.

Deucie edged her blue roan down the trail. At times the going was so narrow that her left stirrup rubbed the rising bluff on that side. The drop-off was invisible. Clouds met the edge of the trail like a deep carpet. There was ice underfoot as the roan's uncertain motions attested. Marsh yelled at Deucie.

'Damnit! We'll never get off the mountain at the pace you're going.'

Beside Deucie, Bedel muttered through his red beard, 'We won't get off at all if we go any faster.'

The heavy-legged gray he rode was two hands taller than Deucie's mount. A deep-chested animal, undoubtedly purchased and trained for quick escapes and long-riding, it was nevertheless not mountain-bred and was ungainly and nearly uncontrollable in this unfamiliar environment.

Bedel yelled back over his shoulder once more, 'I'm telling you, Marsh—'

Then Deucie saw the big gray horse's right hind leg slip as it failed to find purchase on the icy trail. It half reared in fright. Bedel's eyes were suddenly as wide as the terrified horse's; the bearded man thrashed at the reins, but they gave him no control over the skidding animal.

Once one leg was gone over the side there was no chance for Bedel's horse, and with Bedel hooked in the saddle, the big animal started a slow-turning fall into the mass of low clouds. Bedel did not yell out or scream. He was simply there one moment and gone the next, falling invisibly through the concealment of the storm clouds. Deucie waited, counting the seconds, and finally there came a single distant sound, muffled like a muted stroke on a funeral drum.

'That's it,' she heard Kyle Handy say. 'We've

got to go back.'

'He's right, Marsh,' Jeremy said. His bearish eyes showed deep fear. Maybe he had the nerve to stand up against a man in a gunfight, but to go this way – as Bedel had – was something he had no stomach for.

Marsh was long in answering only to maintain his position of leadership. There was nothing to consider. They could not move ahead, and to delay returning was to chance a slide behind them. If that were to happen they would spend the brief remainder of their lives trapped on the ledge in a driving snowstorm. Deucie saw him nod.

'All right. We head back to the cabin.'

With infinite care Marsh backed his horse to the wide spot on the trail where there was room enough to turn the animal. He led the way up through the blinding storm, moving at a cautious pace. Their own tracks were nearly erased by the constant snow and the land was darker yet, enmeshed in the twist and thrust of the storm.

No one spoke. Deucie rode in frozen silence. Her teeth chattered and her fingertips had gone numb. Her toes were only a memory. The little roan battled on gallantly, moving with more will now, perhaps knowing that he would be returned to the sanctuary of his warm barn.

The flats seemed impossibly distant, but an hour's suffering brought them into the pines. The trees were heavy with snow, bleak and dark against the endless white background. But the wind was immediately cut by their ranks. It was winter-dark among the pines, but they could see the trail more easily without the sting of wind-whipped snow in their eyes. They plodded on toward the flats and the house beyond.

Deucie glanced up as Celia, riding at her side, rode near enough to nudge her horse with her own. She thought that weariness had caused it and she opened her mouth to warn Celia off, but she was too late. Celia flipped up the flap of Deucie's coat and before Deucie could react, her cousin had snatched the Remington revolver from its holster. Deucie grappled with Celia, but her horse side-stepped away. Celia slapped spurs to the flanks of her bay horse and waved the pistol in the air maniacally. She rode her horse directly at Kyle Handy who turned in astonishment to see the woman with the gun charging at him, her voice a shrill cry merging with the shriek of the wind.

'I've got you now, you lying dog!'

Celia squeezed the trigger twice and the violent echoes of the shots rattled through the pines as Kyle Handy dropped from his horse's back to tumble to the snowy forest floor.

SEVEN

Deucie sat rigidly in her saddle, as astonished as Kyle Handy. She saw the other men rein in their horses, grab for the pistols beneath their coats, heard them curse and shout. Deucie herself reacted more quickly than thought. She heeled the little blue roan hard, and the surprised pony leaped into a dead run, racing a mad course through the close ranks of the pines. No shots pursued her, and glancing back once she saw no mounted men taking up her trail. She rode on, weaving a twisting course through the trees. She had ridden barrel races many times in rodeos on that little horse and it could cut and change directions like a cat. No one back there had the experience or the horse to catch her, and she knew it. Still she rode until the roan, already weary from the trek on the mountain trail, was exhausted. She would not let him founder and besides, the fear had fallen away from her with the distance covered. At a walk they moved on carefully, keeping to the surrounding cover of the trees.

She had to keep moving, she knew that. But where? Not back to the cabin, for surely the outlaws would return there. She had to find a way to locate Dan, to make sure he was all right. Then together they could perhaps slip down the north slope and back to town. John Highslip might not like riding, but he would have to gather a posse and ride up on Shadow Mountain now that murder had been done here.

The roan walked with its head low and Deucie herself was weary. Weary and cold. She swung down from the pony to give it a rest and leaned her back up against the rough trunk of a wood-pecker-pocked cedar tree. She closed her eyes, but that caused her to grow dizzy. The wind, muted as it was by the forest, was nevertheless cutting-cold. She picked up the lead to the roan and started trudging on, her boots crunching over the snow spread across forest detritus.

He was waiting just ahead.

Stepping out from behind a massive, lightning-struck pine tree he strode toward Deucie. There was no gun in his hand, but he didn't figure he would need it. His face was hard and weathered. His left arm was immobilized. Deucie halted, her blue eyes wide with fear.

Dallas French thought he had found his woman. The long search had been worth it.

'Let's go, Celia,' he said, grabbing the roan's reins from her hand, 'your daddy's waiting for you.'

Deucie was stunned. She had never seen the blond-haired man before, but she knew he was someone to be feared. He had a hungry-wolf look and wore his gun in a way an ordinary cowhand never would – slung low and tied down. His arm, she saw, had been injured. He was hatless in the cold.

'I'm not Celia,' she said, reacting to his words.

'No, you're her twin,' he answered caustically.

'No, I'm her cousin!' Deucie objected. The blond man's expression didn't change.

'Sure. There's a whole flock of you little blonde girls running around up here in this weather. Get aboard that roan, Celia. I'm taking you down the mountain. Don't argue with me – there's eight hundred dollars in this for me, and though I won't hurt you bad, you will find it goes a lot easier on you if you co-operate with me. Do you understand me, girl?'

'I'm telling you. . . .' she protested again, but there was no one there to back her up and the man seemed half-crazed with the fever of his wounds. He looked to be what he was – dangerous and desperate – as he waited, bleeding, for her to obey. What was there to do? As Dan had told her, you never argue with the man with the gun. She replied miserably, 'All right. Let's get going.'

Behind Deucie the uproar among the riders had died down. Jeremy was hunched down over Kyle Handy, examining his wound.

'She got him in the neck, but not bad. Second shot must've missed.'

Marsh was afoot, holding Celia with one gloved hand. He shook her violently. 'What did you have to go and do that for!'

'I hate him!'

'Bandage him as best you can, Jeremy,' Marsh said. 'I wouldn't care if he died except we have to have the both of them to make this plan work. The girl can't be marrying a ghost.'

'I'll never marry him!' Celia spat. Marsh shook her again, hard enough to rattle her teeth.

'Oh, you will, girl. If you don't we'll bury you and *he'll* marry a ghost once we get to Carver Springs. It won't take much to replace you,' Marsh said, his eyes narrowing evilly. 'We'll give some bar girl a bottle of whiskey and twenty dollars and she'll be happy to stand in for you. Think it's a big joke. With Kyle and us – your two brothers – there, no judge will suspicion a thing.'

'My father—'

'Your father won't matter any more, don't you understand that! You be good if you want to stay alive.'

'The other girl, Deucie's, gone,' Jeremy said. The ape-like man looked worried.

'So? What's she going to do?' Marsh demanded. 'We don't need her. We needed her to lead us down that trail, but that's out now. She was just baggage.'

'Featherskill—'

'He's out of it too, isn't he? What does he care about these two? He wasn't willing to hunt them for Amos Corbett. He only wants that Deucie girl back – well,' Marsh said, looking across the snowbound forest, 'he's got her back. Throw Handy over his saddle. We're heading for the ranch house. And smile, Jeremy. Your share just got a little larger; Bedel won't be needing his cut now.'

Dan Featherskill's head came up and he halted the black horse, looking downslope grimly. He had heard two shots. 'Now what did those mean?' he asked the black who shuffled his feet, steam rising from his overheated body. It could have been anything, but the crack of the weapon was lighter than that of a .44. None of the outlaws carried anything smaller. Could it have been Deucie's .36 Remington? He shook his head again. What would she have been shooting at? She was smart enough not to fire it at men who outgunned her no matter the reason. And there had been no answering fire.

Still, it did not bode well, and he found his stomach tightening, his whole body tensing as he started the black forward again, moving in the general direction of the shots.

The storm was proving to be unpredictable. There would be heavy snowfall and a roaring north wind at one minute and then relative calm with thunder rumbling to the east. The clouds swarming the mountain obscured all vision at times and then again a tunnel of illumination would bore its way through the opacity and

Featherskill was able to see a hundred yards or more across the glittering snowfields.

He rode a randomly chosen course, continuing on toward the head of South Pass. He had no doubt that the outlaws would try to make their escape that way now that the western trail was lost to them. The snow began in earnest again and he lowered his head and guided the black toward the stand of jack pines and cedar trees to his right. Riding on, the wind slinging light broken branches from the trees, dropping pine cones on him, shrieking as the occasional impulsive gust picked up, he came suddenly upon the tracks of the horsemen.

Frowning, Featherskill reined the black in. What was going on here? He studied the tracks, stepping from the black's saddle for an even closer look. The horses were heading back toward the meadow, the Campbell house.

Had they found the pass blocked or perhaps lost their way? It seemed likely – in this weather it would take courage along with a large amount of luck to make it down the mountain. He lifted his eyes toward the meadow, hidden behind the thick timber, and put his hands on his hips, frowning even more deeply as he studied the vanishing tracks.

Four horses only. He was certain of that. The tracks were plain in the three inches of snow. What was not clear was whose horses these were. The tracks were indistinct, of course, and an army-shod bay's sign read no different than a cow pony.

Four horses where there should be six. And following on the heels of the two shots he had heard from a light revolver. Did that mean Deucie had escaped, had killed one of them? He glanced in the opposite direction, toward the head of the trail, a mile or so distant. It made no sense for him to backtrack that far when he might find no indication of what had happened as still more snow fell, smothering all signs of passing, of struggle.

He had to follow the four riding toward the house, hoping that Deucie was among them, that she was well. If they had harmed her in any way . . . he could not allow himself to dwell on that. Through the confusion of the storm, he turned the weary black northward, toward the Campbell ranch.

Inside the cabin the men stamped the snow from their boots and shed their heavy coats. They had thrown Kyle Handy roughly on the sofa. He was bleeding from the neck, and he gave an occasional moan, but he seemed not to be in a serious condition. All the same, Marsh told Celia, 'You'd better boil some water, make some bandages and see to your boyfriend.'

'Let him die!' Celia spat.

'I'll do it, Marsh,' Jeremy said. No one heard him mutter, 'It's going to be an interesting honeymoon.'

With his buffalo coat removed Jeremy looked slightly less like a bald-headed ape, but only a little. Marsh stood combing the frost from his beard with his fingers as the fire, fresh logs added, sparked and curled brightly.

'We're out of luck if the kid can't ride,' Jeremy commented.

Marsh nodded and then shifted his small dark eyes to Roxanne who sat rocking gently in her chair.

'That old lady's getting on my nerves,' he muttered.

'What do you expect her to do!' Celia asked. Marsh ignored Celia as he had been doing ever since they had met. Celia was only a piece of the plan, to be preserved, not to be heeded.

'Where do you think her cousin got to?' Jeremy asked, returning from the kitchen with a blue enamel pan filled with water. He placed the pan over the fire and waited for it to heat, holding it with a rag.

'I don't know. I expect she high-tailed it down the north slope, back to town.'

'Doesn't that worry you?'

'Why? It'll take her all day to get there – if she makes it. What's she going to tell them down there? That you and me are doing what Corbett hired us to do – bring back Handy and his daughter?'

'I guess you're right. I hadn't thought of it that way,' Jeremy said, rising as the water began to boil.

Kyle Handy was watching them with morose eyes. It was hard to tell what he was thinking. Celia knew. Kyle wanted always to be the man in charge, and he was no longer. Somehow he had relinquished command to Marsh, and now the success of his plan was totally dependent on the big man's whims.

They heard Roxie begin to move more agitatedly, rocking more quickly, waving her hands violently, and Marsh barked at Celia, 'Do something to shut her up!'

'What am I supposed to do?' Celia snapped back.

'How would I know? She's your aunt, isn't she?'

'No. She's my stepfather's sister. I never had to take care of her. That was Deucie's job. I don't know what she wants.'

'Well, do something. Put her in bed or feed her – something.'

'I said I don't know what she wants,' Celia whined, and she sat down in a wooden kitchen chair, crossing her legs. Her foot began to jerk with her own agitation. Marsh thought, but did not say, that she resembled the old lady just then.

Kyle let out a complaint and Marsh looked that way. Jeremy was squatted beside the wounded man, swabbing at his neck where it joined his shoulder. The rag was bloody from his efforts. 'How is it?' Marsh wanted to know.

'I've gotten worse falling out of bed,' Jeremy said. 'I could use something to put on it, though. There any carbolic in the house, lady?'

'How would I know?' Celia said.

'You aren't worth much, are you?' Marsh said.

'She's worth a cattle spread and gold in the bank,' Kyle Handy muttered. He said it as if that were no longer enough.

'True,' Marsh admitted. He lifted his eyes

110

toward the window. 'Did you hear something outside?'

'No,' Jeremy said, but he rose anyway, crossing to the window, his hand on his gun. He peered out. 'Can't see a thing with that storm. Likely it was the wind you heard. What did it sound like?'

'I don't know.'

'*Featherskill!*'

Their heads jerked around. It was the old woman who had spoken. None of them had heard her speak before, and the astonishment was general. No one replied for a minute. Marsh stared at the old woman, looked again at the window, the snow falling beyond and then grumbled, 'Shut up, old woman.'

'Maybe she's right,' Celia said nervously, leaning forward in her chair.

'There's nothing he can do – if it is Featherskill. Nothing at all.'

'Deucie. . . .'

'No one put a finger on the girl. The rest of this,' Marsh shrugged heavily, 'it's none of his business. I heard him say it myself.'

'That's right,' Jeremy agreed eagerly. 'Besides, Deucie isn't even here!'

Celia said, 'No. But Featherskill doesn't know that, does he?'

Kyle Handy spoke from the sofa. He had managed to sit up, but his pale face showed fatigue and discomfort. 'We don't even know if he's around. Just because that crazy old woman said his name – that's no proof of anything.'

'That's right,' Jeremy said, and then the little ape smiled, 'besides, what do we care, huh, Marsh? Handy here is the one who shot Dan Featherskill and made off with his woman. Maybe we should just toss him outside.'

Handy blanched, but Marsh said, 'No, he's the one with the marriage license.'

'That's true,' Jeremy reflected. 'I suppose this is our fight whether we like it or not.'

'Give him to Featherskill,' Celia urged. 'I can pay you, Marsh. It's *my* ranch we're talking about, remember?'

'I remember,' Marsh said, 'and from what I've learned about you, I can just bet you'd pay us off. One way or the other.'

'I have it all figured out . . .' Celia said in a rush of words, but Marsh again ignored her. The woman was no good. Marsh thought he would have rather trusted his throat to any dance-hall girl in the territory than to this properly brought-up young lady.

'How's the weather?' Marsh asked Jeremy, who

112

was now peering out the window.

'It's lightening up to the north,' he replied. 'And the snow looks thinner. I'd say the storm's broken. Give it an hour or so and we can probably be on our way.'

'I don't see how,' Celia said, and they saw the triumphant little smile on her face and simultaneously heard what she had heard – the drumming of hoofbeats. Rushing to the window himself, Marsh got there in time to see their horses racing free across the snowy valley floor, being driven by a man on a black.

'Featherskill! Damn him!' Marsh shouted. He flung open the front door, unlimbering his Winchester. He fired wildly at the snow-blurred figure escaping through the darkness of the storm and then lowered his gun in frustration.

'That's it,' Jeremy said dully. 'He's got us.'

'He's got nothing!' Marsh said angrily. 'He can't shoot his way in here.'

'He doesn't have to,' Kyle Handy said with his head hanging in surrender to their fate. 'Does he, Marsh? All he has to do is wait now. We're done.'

'Is that what you think, Handy?' Marsh boomed. 'I pity you, boy. No wonder you've ended up in this state.' He glanced meaningfully at Celia. 'You never developed a heart, Handy. We're not stopped, not by a long shot. All Featherskill's done is let us know for certain that he's out there.

'There's still three of us,' the bearded man went on. 'He can't take us all. Featherskill's no magician, just a flesh and blood target. I've got plenty of ammunition. One of these bullets is bound to have his number on it.'

Jeremy was less confident, but Marsh had a point. The man was only human – and from what they had heard, he had been shot up pretty good. Marsh was certainly right in believing they had to go out after Featherskill. Waiting him out was senseless. Featherskill had all the time in the world; they did not.

'Is there a back door?' Marsh asked, looking around.

'No,' Celia said. There was a strange eager light in her eyes as if she was anticipating a blood-letting with pleasure.

'Come on, then,' said Jeremy. 'We'll make our own exit. Are you going to be able to stay alert, Handy?'

'It beats dying.'

'You're right,' Marsh said. 'You hold this house, you hear me? Featherskill does not cross that threshold.'

'He won't.'

'Make sure of it.' Marsh thrust Handy's rifle roughly into his hands. He looked again at Celia, 'And make sure that woman doesn't get behind you with a butcher knife. I want you alive even if she doesn't, bridegroom.'

Having said that, Marsh and Jeremy tramped down the corridor of the house to the back bedrooms. In one of these, the one facing the crescent-shaped pine ridge, there was a high, narrow window. It looked barely wide enough for a man to slither through, but there was little choice. Marsh was determined to meet Featherskill out in the open, not boxed in where Dan could wait and potshoot them at his leisure.

Jeremy was given a hand up, Marsh supporting his boot with his hands forming a stirrup. It was a struggle even after Jeremy had shed his buffalo coat, but the squat gunman managed to wriggle through the window and out onto the snow-covered yard. Marsh tossed Jeremy's coat through the window, stepped cautiously onto the back of a wooden chair and launched himself out into the cold of the day.

Outside they rebuttoned their coats, checked the loads in their sidearms as the gusting wind

115

drove gray snow across the storm-darkened valley. Then at Jeremy's nod, they moved out, Marsh to the north, Jeremy toward the south into the obscuring storm where they meant to track down and kill the only man standing between them and a small fortune.

There could be no mercy and they intended none as they waded through the depths of the storm, searching for Dan Featherskill, snow stinging their cheeks, cold murder in their hearts.

EIGHT

'Well, well,' Dan Featherskill said to himself. They had managed to clamber out of the house through a back window, it seemed. 'So they've decided to come hunting.'

That suited Dan as well as anything. He watched the two shadows wading through the obliterating storm, their movements heavy in the deep snow. Now and then they would be veiled by cloud and snow, but always they reappeared. Perhaps they thought themselves invisible in the storm. True, they were only creeping shadows, but he could follow their progress easily enough.

Sheltered behind the twin flat-topped boulders, he watched their stealthy approach. Snow floated down onto Dan's back, and he became a rounded hump blending with the landscape.

Where was Deucie? When he had slipped into the barn, untied the outlaws' horses and hied them out of there, he had seen at first glance that Deucie's little blue roan was not among them. That could mean a number of things, of course. Deucie may have made a break for freedom, perhaps firing those two shots back in their direction with her Remington to give them pause to think.

Or, it could mean that the roan had foundered, or come up lame, and Deucie had been forced to put the animal down. That would account for the shots as well. If that were the case, she may have then been forced to ride double with one of the bad men. The tracks had been too indistinct in the snow to discover any evidence to show that one of the horses might have been carrying double.

If she had escaped ... there was another horse not accounted for. Had one of them gone to try tracking her down? Featherskill shook his head. There was no way of knowing. He had to continue as if Deucie were being held prisoner in the Campbell house.

They knew. Those men who were now easing their way across the flats, nearing the pine woods, knew what had happened to Deucie.

And they would talk to him. He would see to that.

Holding his fire – they were still far out of accurate range for a six-gun, his only weapon – Dan watched as the stalking men moved into the shelter of the dark forest and were lost to its shadowy depths. He could no longer see them, but still he held the advantage. He knew where they were and they could be tracked. They had no idea if Dan was still even in the area. He might have ridden off with the ponies and even now be moving off the mountain.

No, he thought grimly, they would know that was not the case.

They would know he would not stop until he had found Deucie.

The black horse stood concealed in a stand of scrub oak. Featherskill would leave it there for the time being. Mounted, he would present too large a target silhouette. He preferred things this way. He could move more silently, shoot with more accuracy. He rose slowly from his coverlet of snow and slipped into the woods, a stalking wolf seeking its quarry.

Lightning crackled again, far to the east and a low bellow of thunder shook the earth beneath Featherskill's feet as he wound his way through the maze of great pines, their scent heavy in the air, their needles hidden beneath the snow cushioning his steps.

A flash of color. Featherskill drew up behind a tree trunk, holding his pistol beside his ear, muzzle pointed skyward. He had seen something, indefinite and briefly only, but the color, red, had been certain and no color belonged in the gray-green of the storm-shrouded forest. He found himself holding his breath, his thumb hooked over the curved hammer of the big Colt .44 he held. He did not see the object again, nor the blur of a hunting man moving softly through the forest. He waited, eyes combing the thick stand of trees, his ears alert to every small sound.

There were an amazing number of small sounds, ice breaking a twig as it gathered and weighted the dry wood, pine cones dropping intermittently, the scurrying sound of a confused squirrel, the rustling of the high branches in the shifting wind.

And then, the unmistakable sound of a stick breaking under someone's boot. Featherskill smiled grimly. He had found his man – or rather, one of them. A squat, thick-chested man with a red muffler wrapped around his throat moved forward hesitantly. He was no woodsman, and the slippery footing made his progress uncertain. Featherskill crouched down then, watching as the man grew nearer.

The hunter's expression was uncertain, he looked as if he would have rather been going in the opposite direction, away from menace, but he crept on, prodded by loyalty or perhaps by greed. Dan waited.

When the man was fifteen feet away, Featherskill rose up and stepped from behind the tree, his gun leveled.

'Put it down,' he commanded, and the stocky man, his eyes slowly sliding toward Dan, remained frozen in position, half-hunched forward, his rifle unmoving. Dan repeated his command. 'Drop that rifle, mister.'

'The hell!'

The shout came not from the man in front of Dan, but from someone behind. Dan silently cursed himself for allowing his own attention to flag as he concentrated on the gunman he had in his sights. The second man was more of a woodsman, a more skilled hunter. Another indistinct word was shouted and Dan threw himself to one side just as the gunman's rifle exploded and a bullet from the weapon's muzzle ripped into the bark of the tree beside him, tearing a long furrow in the rough bark, revealing the white meat of the tree beneath.

Dan fired as he rolled, his shot going wild. It was enough to send the second man scurrying for cover. It emboldened the first hunter to drop to one knee and swing his rifle barrel around, drawing a bead on Featherskill's rolling body.

It was the squat man's last mistake. He should have taken cover as had his friend. His rifle was at his shoulder, his eye squinting along the barrel when Dan, firing from his back, shot him through the head.

Dan saw the man fling his arms up, saw his face go momentarily puzzled. Then his body went limp and he pitched face-first into the snow. From behind Dan the second hunter had opened up with his Winchester, but Featherskill had never stopped moving after his first shot. Scrambling wildly he dove into the thin concealment of the underbrush as two more hastily fired rifle bullets clipped wood around him and the booming echoes of the .44-.40 rolled down the mountainside, challenging the voicing of distant thunder with their intensity.

Dan fired once, hastily, across his shoulder, to keep the other man's head down and then continued on his way. Lurching to his feet he dashed for fifty feet or so through the trees, two more searching shots tearing bark from the pines.

Ahead he saw a shallow depression and he leaped into it, scrambling upslope rapidly as the rushing feet of the gunman approached. Mentally Dan counted the remaining bullets in his gun. There were spare shells in his pocket, but he could not now take the time to reload. He had enough rounds in the cylinder, he figured, to take care of business.

'Featherskill!' a voice roared out as Dan continued on his way scrambling up the snowy, brush-strewn gully. Dan refused to answer. The stalking man did not know where he had gone, that was certain. Dan wasn't about to give his position away by responding.

'Featherskill! I know you can hear me!'

Dan exited the gully and crawled forward on his belly until he was concealed in a screen of brush overlooking the shelf of forest below him. He could see a man pressed against a tree, partially concealed and obviously reluctant to advance. The gunman knew that Dan could be anywhere by now and also that his partner was now dead. He was alone in the whirl of the mountain snowstorm cornered by the man he had tracked there.

'We've got no quarrel, Featherskill. Can you hear me? Your girl's all right. I swear it. Why don't we talk this over? Come on out.'

As he spoke, Dan saw Marsh quietly, carefully chamber a fresh round from the Winchester's magazine. His mind was not on conversation, but on killing. Marsh's only reason for calling out was to try to induce Featherskill to reveal himself. Dan was having none of it. He held his position and waited as Marsh finally decided to advance again, moving from cover with his rifle at the ready.

He was near enough now so that Dan could see the bearded man's expression, hungry and cruel. His mouth moved with silent, vicious words. It would have been an easy shot, but Featherskill was no murderer. As Marsh halted, turned half away from him, he rose from the snow like a forest beast, and with his pistol drawn and ready, he spoke.

'If you're serious about talking this over, drop that rifle and we'll have a talk,' Dan said in a low voice.

Marsh span and began firing, levering three rapid shots through the Winchester's barrel. His face was wild with murderous glee. Gunsmoke rose into the dark skies, heavy and acrid, and the rifle's rumble filled the forest with deafening echoes.

Dan raised his Colt and took steady aim as Marsh's wild shots flew past him. His single bullet took Marsh high on the chest and the bearded man staggered back one step, swatting at his heart. Grinning he tried to lift his rifle to his shoulder, but it seemed suddenly too heavy, his arms too frail. His legs began to tremble and his knees buckled under him. His mouth opened as if he would shout one last defiant word, but no sound passed his lips as Marsh twisted and sagged to the snow-carpeted earth, dead in his tracks.

Featherskill walked across the snow to stand over the man for a moment. A man he did not even know. He wanted to feel sorrow, to regret having taken a life, but there was no forgetting that the gunman wished the same for Dan Featherskill. Marsh had come seeking death and he had found it. There was no other end for men like that; they inevitably found what they pursued.

Deucie.

If he wasn't lying, Marsh had said that Deucie was unharmed. Did that mean she was still in the house, being held prisoner? And by how many men? Featherskill carefully reloaded his Colt and holstered it, starting southward, toward where he had picketed his horse.

He was going to have to take the house somehow, knowing that there would be men with guns watching for him. How?

The two men who had come hunting him had not come out the front door, Dan knew. He had been watching. 'Therefore there must be a back window in the house. Dan had never seen one, but then he had never had occasion to go into either of the bedrooms.

That way, then. It was doubtful anyone would be watching. They would be pasted to the front windows, watching the valley floor for the return of their friends. Or for the coming of Dan Featherskill.

He would not disappoint whoever it was that held the house. Deucie was there; he would fight his way in if necessary. And if necessary, fight his way out. Grimly he walked on through the light, swirling snow and the towering dark pines.

The black stood ready, watching Dan's approach curiously. The horse must certainly have been hungry, but it had had a long rest now, and it moved out lightly as Dan began to circle the house, riding toward the crescent ridge above and behind it. No one would see him in this weather, and with luck, no one would see him slip down the bluff on foot and make his way to the rear of the log building.

One thought rode with him as he turned up his collar and bowed his head into the frigid blast of the wind – God help the man who dared to harm Deucie Campbell.

'No more shots,' Kyle Handy said, turning from the window. 'I wonder what happened.'

'Dan Featherskill killed them both,' Celia said just to provoke him. She found herself uncaring; let them all shoot each other up. It no longer mattered to her who won.

So long as, in the end, she was finished with Kyle Handy and his scheming ways. He had grown pathetic in her eyes. The handsome, daring young man who had come to steal away with her from Amos Corbett's ranch was proving himself to be small, frightened and incompetent.

Now, with disdain, she watched the man, his face whiskered, hair uncombed, a bloody rag tied around his neck with bulky knots. His shirt was open, showing a stained undershirt. He continued to watch the window nervously, his hands occasionally twitching when he thought he saw something moving in the storm.

'Why don't you go find out what happened?' Celia said mockingly. 'You can take care of Dan if he's shot Marsh and Jeremy.'

'Shut up,' he grumbled, without looking back at her.

'You don't need them, do you? You never did. You're such a man!'

'I said *shut up*, Celia.'

'I don't care what you say. No one cares what you say. You're nothing, Kyle. You're not even a man.'

'I ought to—'

'Go ahead!' she laughed scornfully. 'You haven't even got the heart for that.'

Her eyes were challenging, her mouth curled with contempt. She knew that he could not shoot her. Killing Celia would mean the end of his plan, would mean that all of this had been for nothing. She found herself almost wishing that he would force her to marry him. What a living hell she would make of his existence.

'He must have got them,' Handy said, glancing over his shoulder at Celia who sat in the wooden chair still, legs crossed at the ankles, head thrown back, mouth agape in a massive yawn. She ignored him now. 'They'd be back if they were alive. There'd be shooting. Maybe all three of them are dead,' he conjectured. 'We'll wait a while. If no one returns . . . we'll go it alone.'

'Where will we go, Kyle?' Celia laughed. 'How will you get me there? You'd have to tie me up and throw me across the saddle to get me on a horse. I'm not going with you, and you can't make me.'

'And I thought you wanted to get out from under Amos's thumb.'

'And end up under yours! No thanks,' Celia replied. 'I would have taken care of Amos one way or the other anyway. Sooner or later.' She heard a faint squeak and turned to face Roxanne who was trying to say something, her eyes fiery with unexpressed anger.

'What's the matter, old lady? Didn't you know that I hate your brother Amos? I do. I despise him. That's why this seemed like a good idea at first. I could see his face when Kyle and I rode back and threw him off the place. With four men and the law on my side I would have done it while I laughed myself sick – sent him out of the territory the same way he came in, broke and desperate. I might have let him have a horse to ride, I— What was that?'

'What?' Kyle was brought to nervous alertness. 'Did you hear something?'

Celia was on her feet. now. 'I'm sure I heard something. Maybe a tree limb brushing the roof.'

'There aren't any trees that close to the house.'

Celia's eyes were fixed on the hallway leading to the back of the house. Now Kyle's gaze went that way too and he nervously raised his Colt. His voice was a rasping whisper.

'Marsh and Jeremy went out that way, through the window.' He looked anxiously at Celia. 'Maybe they decided to come back that way.' The idea was ludicrous, but he clung to it. He preferred it to the alternative.

'Why don't you have a look?' Celia asked, with a harsh laugh. 'Whatever it is, I'm sure you can take care of it, Kyle. You're a big man.'

His lips moved but he did not answer. Found that he could not. Listening, he too heard a sound. Small, indistinct, muffled, as if a squirrel had gotten into the house through the open window and was scuttling across the floor. Maybe that was precisely what had happened! Maybe. . . .

Featherskill stepped into the hallway from the

bedroom and Handy triggered off his Colt three times in rapid succession, his bullets flying wildly into the confined space, smoke curling through the room, roaring echoes rattling their eardrums.

Dan had pulled back into the doorway at the first movement of Kyle's gun hand. Now he emerged again, rolling across the floor, firing up from a prone position as Handy shot again, his bullet singing past, impacting the wall beyond Featherskill. Dan waited, watching the smoke clear, listening as the echoes of the gunfire faded to an eerie silence.

Then he rose. Handy was down, dead against the floor, his revolver still in his grip.

'Anyone else!' he called out recklessly, but the house remained silent. There was only the whispering of the wind in the eaves and a faint, eerie creaking sound. Dan stepped out into the living-room and saw Celia lying on the floor, the back of her head bloody, her eyes open and unblinking. The fire poker lay on the floor next to Roxanne's rocking chair. The old lady rocked backward and forward, eyes intent on the fireplace where still a wisp of flame glowed.

Featherskill holstered his pistol, shook his

head and walked to the hearth. He added two logs to the fire and rose, wiping his hands on his jeans. He replaced the bloody poker in its rack. The unseeing eyes of the woman in the rocking chair followed his movements.

Dan said, 'I've got to find Deucie now, Roxanne.' The old woman remained silent. 'Can you tell me anything to help me? Did they say what has happened to her?'

Dan waited, but there was no answer forthcoming. His lips tightened and he wiped his chin with his grimy hand, 'I'll find Deucie and bring her back, Roxanne. It'll be all right.'

Dan wondered if his words were the truth. Would it be all right ever again for Roxanne? He could feel only vague concern over the woman's dark destiny. Only one thing mattered in his world just then: mattered more than anything had ever mattered before.

He had to find Deucie!

The dead he dragged out to into the barn and covered with a tarp. The burying would have to wait.

Recovering the black, Dan rode slowly away from the house of sorrow. The storm seemed to be breaking now. Here and there Dan saw a patch of brilliant blue sky although snow still fell to the south and east.

He was still able to follow the tracks that had led him to the ranch from near South Pass. His eyes constantly searched the ground, thinking he might have somehow missed the tracks of the blue roan, but he saw none.

Until he reached the pine forest at the head of the South Pass. There he found the spot where the group had halted. Some of them had dismounted, obviously. Boot tracks were evident. And there were signs of mischief.

Frowning, Dan swung down and examined a torn-up muddy area of the clearing. There was evidence that a body had lain in the snow and mud. Dan touched a spot of maroon staining the snow and lifted his fingers, rubbing them together. Blood.

This, then, was where the shots had been fired. But who had done the shooting? He recalled the crude bandage around Kyle Handy's neck and speculated pointlessly. It was doing him no good to consider what might have happened. He led the black in a gradually widening circle until he saw in the mud the tracks of a small horse, moving very fast. The rider, whoever, it had been, had departed at a dead run. Mounting, Dan followed the tracks, studying their veering, weaving motions He smiled faintly.

The blue roan.

It had to be the little cutting-pony's tracks. And Deucie was aboard, riding like a girl in a barrel race. She had done well; the pursuers gave it up after a brief chase and the roan continued on its way through the trees, moving toward the north slope.

She had gotten away! Dan's heart swelled and he rode on more quickly. He would not catch up with her quickly, but she was ahead on the trail somewhere, and he would find her before. . . .

He pulled the black up with a grunt and sat the saddle, staring at the sign smeared into the muddy earth. Deucie had dismounted here.

And she had been met. Large boot prints joined hers and their two horses had ridden on together.

What friend could have found her out here? None. What had happened was only too clear. There was no doubt about it. Dan lifted his eyes to the long land before him and smothered a harsh curse.

Deucie had been taken.

She had made her break for freedom only to

be intercepted and captured once again. Featherskill had thought his search to be nearly at an end. Now he knew that it had only just begun.

NINE

The two riders followed No Name Creek toward the Corbett Ranch, using the saddle-back ridge as their landmark. The creek ran full with run-off from the mountains. The day was bright, the massive banks of clouds quickly dissipating before the rising north wind, a cold escort to their ride.

Dallas French rode in silence. His teeth were clenched with pain. The scratch on his cheek had opened up again and the lower part of his face was masked with scab. He wobbled in the saddle, but his eyes were bright and fixed. Deucie rode her weary little blue roan on, having no idea what to expect once the ranch was reached.

Amos Corbett would not pay Dallas – why

should he? Would the feverish gunman then shoot Corbett down? Or kill Deucie in his angry frustration? There was no telling. She knew nothing of the man she traveled with except for his daunting reputation and the implacable determination he exhibited. He had not ridden all this way, gunshot, to surrender what he considered to be his due.

'How far?' French asked, and his voice was a raspy croak.

'No more than a mile,' Deucie answered, without turning her head. Along the creek now, cottonwood trees grew, casting cold shade on the stream and across their plodding horses. There were few cattle on the range, round-up having been held. Only the very old and the very young. In pens farther along Deucie saw three fine, heavy-bodied bulls; and two milk cows grazed in bovine lethargy among a grove of live oak trees where all of the low growth had been nibbled back or trimmed up. A collie dog ran out to meet them barking and circling the horses.

There was smoke rising from the chimney of the stone house. On the covered porch two rocking chairs sat, swaying slightly in the gusting breeze. There was no sign of a living human being, not in the bunkhouse or in the black-smith's shed, the tall red barn. The corral held two shaggy Texas longhorn steers, two of the first of the cattle driven north to Wyoming Territory. They were aged, dull-eyed remnants of another time. If there were any horses on the place, they were not in evidence.

'You go on ahead,' Dallas French ordered. He himself held his sorrel back a bit and, resting his revolver across the saddle in front of him, waited for her approach to trigger a response from the house.

It didn't take long. As Deucie neared the front porch, the door to the stone ranch house swung open and a bulky, unmistakable figure stepped out onto the porch, shading his eyes with a thick hand.

'Who is it!' Amos Corbett yelled. 'Celia, is it you!' His voice broke off and his hand lowered as he recognized the blond girl on the blue roan. He gathered his voice hospitably. 'Well, Deucie, welcome!'

Then Corbett's eyes caught Dallas French's approach and he made a jerky movement as if he would reach inside the door for a weapon. He halted immediately under the influence of Dallas's cocked and leveled Colt .44.

'Step away from the doorway, Corbett,' French said. 'We're coming in.'

'French! Of course – I didn't recognize you. Where's Feeley?'

'Rotting on the mountain,' Dallas said without emotion. Motioning Corbett away from the door, Dallas French swung down heavily. 'You too,' he said to Deucie, who complied, looping the reins of her horse loosely around the hitch rail.

'Anyone else around?' Dallas asked Amos Corbett.

'The cook and the Mexican went to town for supplies; the kid went hunting. We're alone.'

'Good,' Dallas said. He took a long look around to see for himself before he said, 'Inside, Corbett.'

'Sure,' Amos said cautiously, 'but what's this about?'

'What's it about? Here's your daughter: give me my money.'

'You don't understand.' Corbett blustered, but French prodded him into the house.

'Sit down. You, too, girl,' the gunman said. The fire in the hearth had dwindled to a few dully glowing coals. The room was growing cool. Deucie eased away to sit on a lattice-strap-bottomed chair. Corbett stood in the middle of the room, bullishly, for a moment before he surrendered to French's command and sat down on the overstuffed leather sofa.

'You're making a mistake, Dallas,' Corbett told him.

'No, I'm not.' French bent over at the waist and then straightened up again, holding his belly. His pain was apparent. He backed away and leaned against the stone wall, holding his revolver limply at his side. 'I want my money. Eight hundred dollars. That's what you owe me.'

'This is not my daughter!' Amos Corbett said, half-rising. French lifted his pistol and Corbett sagged back again. Watching Corbett, Deucie could see that there was something the matter with the bluff rancher as well. He was pale and the lines around his mouth were drawn down severely. As she watched, Corbett touched his chest briefly with the palm of his hand. 'Tell him, Deucie!'

'My name is Deucie Campbell,' she told French. His watery eyes gazed mulishly at her. His hair hung in his eyes. To his fevered vision she *was* Celia. The prize he had endured cold and hardship for.

'I'm not waiting any longer,' French warned

them through clenched teeth. 'Cough up that eight hundred, or I'll gun you both down.'

'I tell you, this is not my daughter!' Corbett bellowed. Anxiously then, he asked Deucie, 'Where is Celia, Deucie? What's happened to her?'

'I don't know, Amos. She was all right the last time I saw her.'

'Eight hundred . . .' Dallas French repeated. He was half-bent over again, but the Colt was steady in his hand. Amos Corbett lost his temper.

'You damned fool! I tell you this is not Celia. Look, here's her picture!' He gestured toward a silver-framed daguerreotype of Celia which rested on the end table. Dallas French stepped forward and clubbed the picture away without glancing at it. The frame clattered to the oak floor of the house.

'I'll have the money,' French said, biting off each word. 'I don't care if this is your grandmother. Hand it over or I'll shoot you dead. I've had enough.'

'I'm damned if I will!' Amos shot back and Dallas's eyes narrowed to slits as he raised the gun's barrel so that it was level with Amos Corbett's eyes.

'Mister French?' Deucie said gently. She held up her hands, palms toward him and took two steps in his direction. He shifted the muzzle of his gun and she halted. 'Look here – Dallas – it's true. I'm not Celia. I'm Deucie Campbell. You know, Dan Featherskill's girl? I'm not lying to you.' Deucie smiled and put down her hands. 'Please listen to me.

'You're badly hurt,' she continued. 'If you shoot us you'll never live long enough to make it out of this county. They'll ride you down, Dallas, and they'll hang you. You know they will if you murder a woman.

'We have a doctor in town now. You can make it that far. You have a chance. I know you have a rough background, but you've committed no crimes in this county as yet. You can have your wounds treated and when you're recovered, you can ride off a free man.

'Please,' Deucie pleaded. 'I know you want to live. What is the sense of dying with eight hundred dollars in your jeans? The three of us can live – or the three of us will surely all die.'

'I want the money,' Dallas said, speaking as if his voice rose from the grave.

'Amos!' Deucie shouted in exasperation, 'Give him the money.'

'No,' the rancher said. 'I want Celia.' He spoke not with fury or vindictiveness now, but as one who has grown ill. It was almost a death-bed request. Corbett's head was leaning back against the sofa's back, his flesh as pale as a shroud. He was clutching his chest weakly.

'You two are insane!' Deucie said. 'Why won't you listen. . . ?'

'Quiet!' Dallas's voice was a whiplash. 'Someone's coming.'

He came erect and turned toward the window with a sudden rush of alertness. He was wolfish in his movements as he parted the curtains with his gun barrel and peered out into the yard. Now Deucie, too, could hear the clopping of horse hoofs as someone approached and her heart leaped. She knew who was coming. And he was riding right into an ambush.

'Come here, girl,' Dallas commanded, and Deucie slipped up beside him. 'Is that Dan Featherskill?'

'Yes,' Deucie replied in a whisper so weak it was barely audible.

The black horse made its way heavily across the yard. Riding out of the sun, horse and rider were only a mysterious dark centaur. As they neared, Deucie could see that the black was

143

frosted with the salt of its sweat, weary and heavy-footed. Dan Featherskill had shed his buffalo coat and Deucie saw that one sleeve of his dark-blue shirt had been slit to the cuff and that its tails were missing. Dan's face was dark with the bristle of whiskers and his eyes were sunken. He rode the saddle slumped forward as if with exhaustion.

Dallas still gripped his pistol tightly and Deucie lifted a hand toward his wrist.

'You can't—'

'Shut up!' Dallas snapped. 'I wouldn't shoot him from ambush. You don't know me well. When I shoot a man I look into his eyes before I pull the trigger.'

'He's done nothing to you!' Deucie said.

'Not yet. He might have it in his mind. He's seen our horses out there, so he knows I have you.'

'I'll tell him, explain that—'

'I do the explaining, girl.' Dallas turned those fierce, haunted eyes toward her. 'They say he's fast with a gun.'

'Do they? I don't know,' Deucie said frantically. 'I've never seen him fight like that.'

'Do you suppose he's faster than I am?' the Trinidad gunfighter asked.

'No. I don't know.' Deucie ran her fingers through her fringe, wiping it away from her eyes. 'What's the difference?' A new idea came to her and she said, 'You're wounded, Dallas. It wouldn't be a fair fight.'

'He looks like he's pretty bad off himself,' Dallas said, as he watched Dan through the curtains. Featherskill swung down heavily, gripping the saddle horn for a long minute as he steadied himself on the ground.

'Why?' Deucie pleaded. 'You're teetering on the edge of death now. Why get into a gunfight?'

'Like you say, girl,' Dallas answered, 'I'm already teetering. If I fall – so what?'

Then he reached for the door latch, pausing to turn toward Amos Corbett and say, 'You sit where you are. Don't make a move.'

Amos looked like he couldn't have done anything to stop the fight if he wanted to. He looked as if he, too, were teetering on the rim of an open grave, his face sallow, eyes dimly lighted, hand still clutching his heart.

'Step out ahead of me, girl,' Dallas French said. 'Just in case he's got any ideas of cutting me down before I have a chance to speak my piece.'

Trembling, Deucie reached for the open edge of the door. *Why?* she asked without speaking.

145

But she could do nothing to stop this now, nothing at all. She stepped out into the bright sunlight as Dan, leading the black to the hitch rail, halted in surprise. Dallas French came out now, his gun holstered, and he pushed Deucie roughly aside.

'Dallas French?' Dan enquired. At Dallas's nod, he said, 'That figures. Looks like you're shot up pretty good, French.'

'Yeah, they shot me back there on the mountain. The cowards' way, from ambush.'

'That's what I guessed.' Dan looped the weary black horse's reins over the bent hitching rail and stepped back a little, his hand hovering just above his holstered Colt. 'Is there something you wanted from me, Dallas?'

'I don't know yet. I'm thinking about it.' Dallas wavered on his feet. Perspiration stood beaded on his forehead. 'They say you're a fast man with a gun, Featherskill.'

'Do they?' Dan asked quietly.

'Is it true?' Dallas French wanted to know.

'I don't claim it for myself, French. I've been called a fast-draw artist, but then I've had men call me a dog— that doesn't make me one.'

'Saying. . . ?'

'Saying I don't want to draw on you, if that's

146

what you're asking.'

'I don't want you saying some day that you backed Dallas French down,' the gunman said. He was more than unsteady on his feet. He looked as if the ground was dancing under his boots and he could find no purchase on it. He was a deadly creature, a rattler wanting to strike out at the last moment of its life.

'If you draw,' Deucie said, walking to within an arm's length of the gunman, 'I will find you myself and shoot you, Dallas. More – I'll tell everyone that you gunned Dan Featherskill down without giving him a fair chance. I'll tell everyone!'

Dallas's eyes closed to mere slits. The corner of his down-turned mouth twitched. He kept his attention on Featherskill, watching for the slightest motion of his right hand.

'Is this your woman, Featherskill?' the gunfighter asked.

'Yes. That's my woman, French.'

The gunman's shoulders lifted and then lowered. His hand fell away from his holstered pistol. 'Spunky, ain't she?' Then he said to Deucie, 'Get my pony for me, Spunky. Then tell me where I can find this doctor of yours.'

They watched as Dallas French dragged his

battered body on to the sorrel's back and started it forward through the oak grove, heading away toward town. When he had merged with the shadows and was no longer visible, Dan said, 'I've got to be seeing to my horse.'

Deucie smiled faintly. Featherskill was in no shape for anything. He was barely able to keep his own feet. She slipped beside him and put his arm across her shoulders. Supporting his weight she helped him into the house where Amos Corbett sat staring at them in blank pain from his seat on the leather sofa.

'Is he gone?' Amos asked in a raspy groan.

'He's gone.'

'Saved myself eight hundred dollars,' he said. Featherskill and Deucie both ignored him as they got Dan seated on the chair opposite the rancher. Dan removed his hat, handed it to Deucie and took a deep breath, running his fingers through his hair.

'I've bad news for you, Corbett,' Dan Featherskill said softly. And he told his listeners as much of what had happened as they needed to hear. There was no point in airing all of the dirty details surrounding Celia's death.

Deucie had to sit down, her eyes showed shock and sorrow. Corbett closed his eyes tightly and his broad mouth compressed itself into a tragic line.

'I didn't know how to raise the girl,' he said at last. He wiped his nose on his cuff. Staring at the floor he clenched his hands and told them, 'I didn't know the right things to do, to say.' His eyes lifted. 'You know how I am – one gruff bastard.'

'It's never easy,' Dan said.

'I tried to protect her and instead I turned her away from me. I see that now. But I knew that Kyle Handy was no good. I knew what he was after. Men told me he'd been snooping around where he shouldn't, asking questions about how much the ranch was worth, how many steers we would be pushing to market this year. Then he set out to charm Celia.

'There aren't many young men around,' Corbett said with a sigh. 'And those who came courting, I generally shooed away,' he admitted.

'She was tired of ranch life,' Deucie said.

'I know that. No female company. No dances or parties. That was why she was happy whenever she could spend time with you, Deucie.'

'So it wasn't hard for Kyle Handy to talk her into running off with him,' Dan commented.

'No,' Corbett said wearily. 'And I went wild.

149

People could say what they liked. I know a lot of them thought I just wanted to keep the ranch – but that wasn't it. I wanted to keep Celia around. To have her for a daughter.'

'Bringing her back at gunpoint wasn't the answer,' Dan said. He stood now and looked out the window. Dallas was gone, he knew, but you could never be sure.

'I went crazy!' Corbett said, waving a hand. 'I should never have talked like I did, demanding that you kill Kyle Handy. That was all just madness. And it drove you away from the job, Featherskill. The only man I really trusted to do it right.'

'So you hired Dallas and Brad Feeley.'

'I did. They were raw men, but tough ones. I knew they could do the job.' He paused and breathed in deeply, his hand again going to his chest.

'You ought to have the doctor check your heart,' Deucie said.

'I did once. There's nothing he can do about it,' Corbett said, as if it didn't matter. Not any more. 'I should have known, shouldn't I? That Kyle Handy, as clever as he was, would have taken precautions. That he would have anticipated that I'd send somebody after him. That he'd hire men to back his play.'

'You underestimated him,' Dan said. 'Figured he was just a greedy kid.'

'I wasn't thinking straight.' Amos Corbett's eyes met Featherskill's. They were moist and sorrowful eyes. 'I did love the girl, you see. No matter what anybody thinks. She was all I had.'

Dan and Deucie exchanged a look. Was Corbett being honest with them, or was this just an emotion born out of events, a knowledge of his failing health? It made no difference, Dan supposed.

Corbett sighed again and fixed his eyes on Deucie, 'Well, there's always a silver lining, isn't there? You'll never have to worry about scratching a living on that rock farm of yours again, Deucie.'

Deucie was perplexed. 'What do you mean. Mr Corbett?'

'What do I mean? Why, Celia's dead now, isn't she? Who do you suppose this ranch belongs to now?'

'I don't understand you,' Deucie said. 'Do you, Dan?'

Featherskill shook his head and Corbett explained. 'It's you, Deucie. I saw the will that Celia made out last year. She was angry with me

151

then and she made sure I saw it. She wanted to make sure that I knew that I would get nothing if . . . if anything happened to her. I dunno,' he said gravely, 'maybe she thought I was willing to do her harm for the sake of the ranch, She was wrong, of course!'

His protest seemed too vehement. Dan and Deucie simply nodded agreement. 'She had a will drawn up and she showed it to me. She left all she had to you, Deucie.'

'Why me?'

'Who else was there? She always considered you to be her cousin, her only relative, her only friend. The ranch is yours.' Corbett roughly massaged his scalp with his thick hand. 'All the money they get for selling them cattle over in Kansas will be yours. This house. The chair you're sitting on. You'll be a well-off young lady, Deucie.'

'No,' she answered firmly. 'I didn't build this ranch up from the raw earth. Celia's father started it, Amos, but you are the one who worked it over the years and made it grow.'

'The law doesn't weigh things that way, Deucie. Roxanne and I both came into this country dirt-poor, meaning to make our fortunes as we could. Poor Roxie never made hers; I did, but here it flies away on me.' He rubbed his heart, 'Well, what does it matter? I have no one to leave it to either, and I doubt I'll be around long enough to enjoy it. Now.'

'You're going to stay on here, aren't you?' Deucie asked.

'If you want me to,' Corbett replied uncertainly.

'Of course I do! I have no idea what I should do right now. I have to have time to think. I certainly have no experience in running a cattle outfit. I could learn, I guess – but the mountains are my home, Amos,' Deucie said sincerely. 'It may seem a poor life to you, but I love our mountain valley.'

'I'll stay. If you decide you want me to stay and run the place, of course I will,' Corbett said. He looked at Featherskill and then beyond him, to a different world where the life he wished he had led flourished briefly. Then, rising heavily, Corbett went to the sideboard, unlocked a drawer with a small brass key he kept on his watch chain and returned, wallet in hand.

Opening it, he slipped out eight one-hundred dollar bills. 'Dan – here's the reward. Take it.'

'I did nothing to earn it,' Featherskill said, refusing.

'You came as near as anyone,' Corbett said with a tight smile.

'No, sir,' Dan replied. 'I cannot.'

'Very well! Then – Deucie – this must belong to you.'

'It does not,' Deucie protested, holding up the flat of her hand. 'You will need it, Amos. For day-to-day operations. If you agree to stay and manage the ranch.'

'Yes,' Corbett said with little hesitation. 'I agree to that. All right then,' he nodded, stuffing the bills back into his wallet. 'When the trail crew returns, I'll keep the money from the cattle sale put aside for you.'

Deucie said, 'What I will agree to do, Amos, is to accept a *part* of that money. We'll work out a fair division and draw up a contract for your services as ranch manager later. The one who puts in the bulk of work deserves the bulk of the pay. I have done nothing to raise, tend, feed and drive those steers to market. A few cash dollars are always welcome in the mountains, but the rest is for you. To pay the men, to reinvest in the ranch. Build it up properly, Amos. Make it a spread you, I, everyone can be proud of.'

TEN

'That was fine of you, Deucie, the way you handled business with Amos Corbett. I know you don't believe the old rascal or trust him.'

'What I said was true enough. He has more right to that money than I do. It'll give him motivation to keep the ranch running as it should, won't it? As I said, I sure can't handle it. And I won't leave the mountains.'

They rode on in silence, the black horse and the little blue roan striding easily across the meadows where patches of snow glittered in the sunlight. In the mountains the peaks were newly white-clad, stark and gleaming against the backdrop of blue sky and lazily drifting clouds.

'Dan,' Deucie asked, 'do you think Corbett really had plans to do away with Celia to get ahold of the ranch – was that the reason she made that new will?'

'It could be,' Dan answered. 'A man like Corbett, driven by greed as he was, might have seen that as a logical move. It drove him nearly mad when he thought Kyle Handy had cut his way in ahead of him. Knowing Celia, though, she might have had it done just to infuriate the old man. Who knows?'

He asked her, 'You did mean all that, then, about letting him continue to run the ranch?'

'Oh, yes. He can manage it until the clock catches up with him. It's better for everyone. Of course,' she confided, 'I intend to keep a closer eye on the books than he might like.'

Dan laughed. 'I would.' He smiled at the slender blonde woman. The heavy braid down her back hadn't been arranged for a while. He wondered if she would let her hair loose, to drift free in the breeze if he asked her. There was a smile playing around her mouth and amusement in her eyes. He wanted to ask the cause of her humor, but did not.

They splashed across No Name Creek and halted among the sycamore trees to rest their mounts. Deucie stood with her arms crossed beneath her breasts, looking to the high country, to Shadow Mountain. Without glancing at Dan, she asked, 'What you told Dallas French, did you mean it, Dan?'

'French?' Dan's eyes narrowed in puzzlement. 'What was that, Deucie? I said a few things to him.'

'You know,' she said, and now she did turn toward him, lowering her arms. She looked up into his eyes and reminded him, 'When he asked if I was your woman, you told him that I was. Did you mean that, Dan?'

Dan hesitated. The question had been unexpected. Those moments can cause a man's wits to stumble. He finally answered, 'Yes, Deucie. I thought you always knew that.'

'Oh, I thought I did, too, Dan,' she replied. 'But it's not much use knowing you belong to a man when he's never around to tell you that. When he's off riding here and there trying to find an early grave for himself. It's not a great comfort to a woman, Dan.'

'Deucie . . . I'm not cut out for that life of yours. This is a wild and free, great country.' He gestured widely with his arm. 'I need to feel part of it all.'

'I see,' Deucie said quietly.

'You always knew that, Deucie.'

'Yes. We hope, you know. We women. But just look at you, Dan Featherskill! You're dirty and scabbed and battered and bruised. You came within a split-second of getting shot by that Trinidad gunfighter! And to boot, you didn't make a penny out of the whole adventure!'

Dan was thoughtful. 'Do you think that Dallas French could have taken me in a fair fight?'

'Couldn't he?'

'He might have had a chance,' Dan said, and they both smiled. She laughed then and fell into his arms and he held her. 'Would you let your hair down?' he murmured.

'For my husband,' Deucie said brightly, drawing back to look up at him.

'Deucie . . . I can't be a damned farmer!'

She went on tiptoe and kissed him lightly on the lips. 'I never asked you to be a farmer, Dan,' she reminded him. 'I only asked you to settle down.'

He was weakening. He knew that and she felt it. She kissed him again, teasingly and he answered, 'It truly is a wild and free country out there, Deucie,' he said looking to the far mountains. 'A glorious land. But maybe I just don't need such a big chunk of it as I thought.'

'Is that your answer, Dan?'

'As close to one as I'm going to give you,' he said. 'What's yours?'

And her fingers went to her braid and she unfastened it, letting her golden hair fall free across her shoulders, the breeze shifting it like a silken promise in the bright sunlight.